THE PURLOINED LETTER OPENER

A LAKE HOPE MYSTERY

LEAH R CUTTER

KNOTTED ROAD PRESS

Reviews
It's true. Reviews help me sell more books. If you've enjoyed this story, please consider leaving a review of it on your favorite site.

Come someplace new…
Are you a traveler? Do you enjoy exploring strange new worlds, new cultures, new people?

Journey into the various lands envisioned by Leah Cutter.

Sign up for my newsletter and I'll start you on your travels with a free copy of my book, *The Island Sampler*.

I will never spam you or use your email for nefarious purposes. You can also unsubscribe at any time.

http://www.LeahCutter.com/newsletter/

ALSO BY LEAH R CUTTER

Forgotten Gods

A Wind Blown Torment

A Stone Strewn Clash

A Sea Washed Victory

Tanish Empire Trilogy

The Glass Magician

The Desert Heart

The Ghost Dog

The Cassie Stories

Poisoned Pearls

Tainted Waters

Spoiled Harvest

Bloodied Ice

The Witch's Progress

Circle of Air

Circle of Water

Circle of Fire

Circle of Earth

Seattle Trolls

The Changeling Troll

The Princess Troll

The Fairy-Bridge Troll

The Troll-Demon War

The Troll-Human War

The Troll-Troll War

The Shadow Wars Trilogy

The Raven and the Dancing Tiger

The Guardian Hound

War Among the Crocodiles

The Clockwork Fairy Kingdom

The Clockwork Fairy Kingdom

The Maker, the Teacher, and the Monster

The Dwarven Wars

The Chronicles of Franklin

Franklin Versus The Popcorn Thief

Franklin Versus The Soul Thief

Franklin Versus The Child Thief

Huli Intergalactic - Science/Space Fantasy

Origins

The Strawberry Girl

Contemporary Fantasy

Siren's Call

The Immortals' War

1

———

*L*ydia Marsh sighed as she looked out over her customers that morning who sat in her teashop-restaurant, *Nip and Bud*. Over half of the dozen small round tables were empty, despite it being June and the height of tourist season in the heart of wine country in Central Washington.

Of course, Lydia's mind leaped to the worst possible scenario—that she'd received a scathing review on Instagram and that no one would come to her restaurant, teashop, or B&B ever again. She forced herself to take a deep breath, smelling the rich coffee as it were, stepping back from the edge, telling herself that she was being silly, everything was just fine.

Despite the lack of customers that morning—there would be a line out the door if all her fantasies came true—Lydia couldn't see one thing that she'd change in the dining room. It was a reflection of her as well as her place, a mix of old-fashioned, modern, and eclectic.

Brilliant morning sunshine streamed in through the restored store-front windows, opposite from where she stood behind the counter, giving the original hardwood floors a warm, golden glow. To the right, chic white- and rose-colored graphic wallpaper highlighted the area, making it a focal point for the room. Floating shelves set asymmetrically continued the modern theme. They were filled with modern as well as antique teapots that Lydia had collected over the years. A cozy fireplace (currently unlit) was tucked into the back corner on that wall, the brick mantel painted white, giving it a bright yet homey appearance.

A set of stairs leading to the two upper floors rose up on Lydia's left, with a tiny (but always spotlessly clean) restroom built under it. Directly across from the stairs was the tall glass door, leading to the quiet street outside.

Tucked in past the staircase was a small gift shop where Lydia sold tourists maps and books about the area, as well as knickknacks, like hand-painted coasters, *Nip and Bud* branded coffee mugs and wine glasses, beautiful tea sets, small bottles of local honey in hand-blown glass bottles, as well as other things that made her heart happy, cute collectables that no one else in the area had. She also had a small collection of local agates and crystals that had been found in or near Lake Hope itself. Some of the trinkets she sold—like the letter openers or the key chains—were partially made out of the gorgeous purple agates found in abundance in the area.

Lydia took another few moments from behind the counter, a nice barrier between her and the few customers, a place where she could collect herself and just breathe. Behind her was the coffee maker filled with a dark roast that she adored. Built-in shelves were behind that, part of the original store that had been here back in the 1900s. Glassware, mugs, cloth napkins, little pitchers for cream, drawers for silverware, everything conveniently placed, no wasted space or items, just what she needed for the finger food she served.

Beyond the wall was the small kitchen which had been converted from a storage area sometime in the 1950s. It had a well-worn single counter for prep to which she'd added a built-in cutting board, a finicky flattop grill that she was going to have to replace one of these days, an industrial sink and sanitizer in the corner, and a walk-in refrigerator at the far end.

Looking out over the dining room again, Lydia tried to content herself with what was there. More than one of the empty tables showed signs of having been recently occupied. Maybe more people would come by for lunch. It wasn't even ten yet. She didn't need to worry.

Lydia gave herself a shake, feeling her long dark braid swinging between her shoulder blades. She readjusted one of the bobby pins, making sure that any wisps of hair were firmly in place. Lydia's hair style was practical for the work she did, as was the rich blue polo shirt she wore that fit comfortably across her wide shoulders and chest. As Lydia was all leg, she only tucked in her shirt when she wanted people to notice her. Today she wore comfortable khaki shorts that came to just above her knee, with comfortable sneakers and cute green-and-black tiger-striped socks. (Life was too short to ever wear boring socks.)

Two of her favorite locals were sitting in her restaurant. They'd both paid "table rent" as it were, ordering more than just coffee and giving her a good tip.

Dennis Solomon, the local investment broker who always dressed as if he were on his way to the golf course, sat reading his morning paper beside the fireplace, in one of the comfy wing-backed chairs. He had on a pale-orange argyle knit-sweater vest that looked as though he'd special ordered it from a vintage shop. Of course he would—he excelled at making money, not just for himself but for his clients. Lydia was quite pleased with the fact that despite running a B&B

that was always needing repairs, she still had something of a nest egg, as well as emergency funds.

Tracy Stevenson, another local, typed furiously on her laptop also against the far wall underneath the teapots, out of reach of the sunlight, pounding on the keys as if they had somehow offended her. It was much better on the mornings like this than when she sat and stared out the window morosely, as if mourning the unfaithful lover she frequently compared her muse to. She was a carrot-top, with pale skin that she claimed would burn under a 120-watt bulb, and always wore unfortunate red tops or red dresses. Lydia frequently had to fight off the urge to pull the other woman to the side and point out that just because she *was* a redhead didn't mean that she should necessarily *wear* red.

Lydia was proud of the restraint she'd shown so far. It really wasn't her place to give fashion advice, as much as she might want to. The world had not seen fit to make her queen of everything. Not yet.

She did know that she had a good eye, however. She'd been taught by the best—her two gay uncles, Ed and Alan, who were heavily into all things fashionable and who followed the pulse of all the trends. She'd spent every summer with them in New York while she'd been a teenager. They still sent her articles about the latest designer collections, complete with bitchy commentary. They also regularly sent her photos of the latest antics of their cat, Poe.

In addition to the locals in the dining room, a tourist couple also sat there, directly in front of Lydia, still mooning over each other. They had spent the night in one of the rooms Lydia rented upstairs and had reserved a spot on the local winery tour bus that would leave at ten. They were on their honeymoon. Lydia had a bet with herself that they wouldn't actually make the tour, as they'd be back in their room celebrating their new love.

That left one other customer. Schooner Thomas, the retired principal of Lake Hope High School, who had taken up grouchy residence in the very center of the room. Lydia frequently wondered if his wardrobe had been inspired by men's suits of the 1930s, with the double-breasted vests and jackets, the wide ties, and the suspenders. Unfortunately, none of it looked good on Schooner. He was tall and scrawny as an old-fashioned scarecrow, his bald head and wisps of white hair around the edges just adding to the effect. The wide black tie he wore looked more like a bib. His suspenders were old, yellowed, and frayed, and looked as though they might suddenly break, at which point, Schooner's pants would hit the floor, as he had no butt or hips to speak of.

He sipped loudly at his coffee, probably too deaf to hear the noise he made. He never ordered any food. He just got plain brewed coffee and filled his cup at least a dozen times if Lydia left the pot out. Though his attention was fixed on the book in front of him, he radiated displeasure like a dark cloud.

There wasn't anything Lydia could do or say to him, though she was certain that he'd started coming to her shop in the mornings this year just to drive away her customers. According to her best friend Patrice Skahonish, who ran the bakery down the street, Schooner had no use for "loose" women like Lydia, women who were not only divorced but still single and not under the proper control of any menfolk.

While Schooner was unpleasant to most people, he'd never been discourteous to Lydia to her face, so she couldn't just kick him out.

Though some days, like this morning, she'd really like to.

The door leading outside opened, the bell hanging above the lintel ringing merrily. Three tourists walked in tentatively, all in their early twenties, two men and a woman. They looked first to the right, at the little gift shop, then to the left, toward the dining room.

Misty abruptly popped up from behind the counter in the gift shop, where Lydia hadn't seen her. Good. While Lydia was okay with people, even with tourists, the primary reason she'd hired Misty was so that she didn't actually have to deal with them most of the time. Whereas Misty actually seemed to like everyone.

Misty cheerfully greeted the visitors, asking about their morning and putting them at ease, as she always did. Seemed they wanted coffee to go—they were going on the winery tour bus as well.

Misty gave Lydia a wink as she walked past, heading to the coffee bar behind the counter. Misty was barely five foot tall, with coarse brown hair, light-brown skin, and a perpetual smile. Though Misty was fifteen years older than Lydia, which made them fifty-three and thirty-eight, respectively, Misty felt even older, and the comfort she gave always felt grandmotherly. She was the opposite of svelte, being round everywhere, but she wasn't overweight, or not grossly so. She was comfortable in her own skin, and made everyone else feel the same way.

However, Misty also gave Lydia a hip check as she'd passed, getting Lydia to move and start clearing tables. If Misty was doing her job, it was probably about time Lydia actually went about doing hers as well, instead of complaining about the lack of customers, even if she was only doing it in her head.

Lydia picked up her empty dish bucket, then checked in on the honeymooning couple, reminding them of the time the bus was leaving. They blushed and sighed and left promptly, probably to sneak in a quickie before their bus departed.

Ah, young love. It was one of the reasons why Lydia

offered honeymooners special deals. Though Lydia had no prospects herself, that didn't mean she couldn't live vicariously off other people's relationships.

Lydia filled her dish bucket with the debris from the formerly occupied tables, nodding at Schooner when he raised his coffee cup, obviously wanting her to fill it yet again.

Maybe she should raise the price of just a cup of coffee by a quarter, but then offer a quarter discount when coffee was purchased with a muffin or some other pastry, all lovingly baked by Patrice.

Though that wouldn't stop Schooner from coming in. He'd just complain louder about her prices behind Lydia's back. He was one of the original investors in a local winery and had accumulated quite a bit of money over the years, never spending any of it. His house up on the hill was a disgrace, the roof needing repairs, the drab wooden shingles needing paint, and the yard a mass of dandelions and weeds.

Part of why Schooner had no use for "loose" women was because his own wife had divorced him when Lydia had been a teenager, leaving him alone to raise their poor son, Bernard.

Lydia had gone to school with Bernard. He'd been one—maybe two?—years behind her. He'd never really registered with her, except for her to feel sorry for him.

No one deserved Schooner Thomas as a father, let alone as their single parental figure.

After Lydia bussed the dishes to the kitchen, she wiped her hands off before going back out into the dining room, carrying the coffee pot and offering refills to her remaining guests. Tracy barely registered that Lydia was there as she conducted her invisible orchestras before pounding on the keyboard some more. Dennis gave her a quick smile and a quiet, "Thank you," for her offer.

Schooner merely sniffed at her, as if to say, "About time."

Lydia kept her smile firmly in place. Everyone else who came to her establishment regularly was a delight. And it wasn't just Schooner keeping people away that morning. No one in town had had a full complement of tourists that week. It was just how the season went. Sometimes you were astonishingly busy. Sometimes, even when you were supposed to be full, you weren't.

Lydia went back into the kitchen to start cleaning and getting everything prepped for lunch. Misty could handle the front. She'd come back and ask for help if she needed. And Lydia would hear the bell on the door if anyone else came in.

The hum of the industrial washing machine/sanitizer and the smell of lemon soap soon had Lydia smiling again. Despite Schooner and the vagaries of her business, she really was lucky. She had good friends, a good career, and if she got lonely some nights, that was okay.

She had tools for that, as well as sound advice from Ed and Alan regarding self-care.

2

"And then there was a buck!" Alice exclaimed as she started folding one of the sheets. "Six points! I counted them all. All by myself," she assured Lydia.

"Good for you!" Lydia said, nodding in encouragement. Alice was developmentally disabled. It showed in her round face and constantly surprised expression. She was sweet and a really hard worker. She'd grown up on a farm just outside of town with parents who adored her and did their best to take care of her. They were some of Lydia's most frequent customers, stopping and having lunch, even on the days Alice didn't work.

Alice helped Lydia clean the eight guest rooms on the top two floors of the B&B. Alice worked Thursday through Monday, coming at 1 PM like clockwork. It had taken Lydia a bit of time to train Alice, but once she'd learned the routine, Lydia couldn't have asked for a better cleaner. Though Alice was in her late twenties, according to her parents she was developmentally somewhere between the ages of eight and ten.

It helped that Alice was really strong. She'd always helped

her parents out on the farm. She could effortlessly switch piles of wet linens between the washer and dryer, even when Lydia was doing a deep clean and washing all the blankets and covers.

They stood that morning in the laundry room, which was on the first floor, down the hallway past the stairs. The laundry, along with Lydia's rooms next door, weren't part of the original building. When Lydia had originally bought the place four years before, she had taken out a second loan to cover the additional building costs. Then she'd splurged and put in a double set of industrial washers and dryers.

It had been one of the best investments she'd ever made. They were huge, easily four feet across, front loading, and stacked one on top of the other in the small room. They hummed loudly, making it impossible to listen to music when she was doing laundry. But having two sets meant that it only took a couple of hours for her to wash and dry every linen in the entire establishment. Being able to turn over the rooms that quickly meant that she could frequently accommodate guests who checked in early.

That was one of the things that always delighted Lydia, and why she enjoyed running a B&B. While she wouldn't call herself a "people person," it gave her a great sense of satisfaction to provide good hospitality to her guests. Her B&B was highly rated on all the tourist sites. Guests frequently commented on social media about the little touches she provided for them, such as the welcome basket in every room (complete with complimentary coffee, tea, and chocolate), the flights of wine that she'd offer at the restaurant once a week during the summer (so people could continue to taste some of the best of the local vineyards), as well as local handmade soaps.

When Alice and Lydia finished doing laundry, they climbed the stairs to change over the rooms. It was Friday afternoon and all but one of the rooms was rented that evening. Lydia wasn't worried about that one last vacancy—chances were someone would just drive by and ask if they had any rooms available. That happened all the time in the summer.

Alice cleaned the bathroom while Lydia made the queen-sized bed. The two larger rooms on each floor had an ensuite, while the other two shared a bathroom. They were in the Cornflower room, which was done in shades of blue. (All the rooms were named after edible flowers that Lydia frequently served in teas.) The bed took up most of the space, with a small armoire in the corner with hanging space on one side and drawers on the other. A flat-screened TV hung from the wall above the cute, antique desk that Lydia had refinished herself, removing the ugly sage-color paint and letting the natural cherry wood shine.

"My cousin Mitch is coming for the weekend," Alice announced as she finished moping the bathroom floor.

Lydia grimaced, glad that Alice couldn't see her. Alice's parents considered anyone single to be living only half a life. (With the exception of their daughter, of course, who had fortunately never shown signs of being interested in anyone.)

Luckily, it was June. Tourist season was in full swing. Lydia didn't have time to go to a dinner or any other event that Alice's parents would arrange so that she and Mitch could spend an evening together.

While Mitch was perfectly fine, he wasn't her type. Though Lydia wasn't exactly certain what her type was, she knew Mitch wasn't it. He was tall and blond and overly intellectual. She wanted someone who wouldn't mind getting their hands dirty.

Plus, Mitch lived in Seattle and worked as a video game historian, whatever the heck that meant. Like Tracy, he was also a writer. Unlike Tracy, he'd never managed to finish even a single novel, while Tracy made her living from her writing.

"We're going to have a picnic on Tuesday!" Alice announced. "Mama showed me the basket and promised that I get to help pack it."

"That's wonderful," Lydia said. Hopefully they'd be going someplace shady—Eastern Washington in June was very warm. Scorching hot would arrive sometime after the fourth of July.

"You could come with," Alice slyly suggested.

"I still have to work," Lydia said. It was the truth, after all. It wasn't that she didn't take any time off—she just wouldn't really have a full day to herself from now until October or November, when the tourist season finally drew to a close.

"You could take the day off," Alice said. "Papa says you work too hard."

"That's probably true," Lydia said. "But when was the last day your papa didn't work on the farm?"

"He always works!" Alice exclaimed. She popped her head out of the bathroom. "Mama too! That's why we're all going on a picnic together. So we don't always work."

Lydia blinked, surprised. That didn't sound like Alice's parents at all. Like most of the folk around here, they didn't know how to take a vacation. That was for tourists and such.

"I'm really glad they're doing that, then," Lydia said. She would have to remember to check with Patrice later, see if she'd heard anything about Alice's parents. Hopefully everything was okay and they were really just indulging their daughter.

"You could also take the day off," came a deep voice from behind Lydia.

"You first," Lydia said, turning and smiling at her dad. She walked over and kissed his cheek.

Her dad still smelled of the bay leaf aftershave he'd used since he'd been a teenager himself, along with the warm smell of a fresh cotton shirt. He wore a light blue T-shirt today, along with jeans. Mom had a thing for laundry. She loved doing it—considered it her artform. Lydia sometimes wondered about her mom.

Before her father had retired, Emerson Marsh had worked as an insurance broker, setting people up with the right policy for them, as opposed to working for a single company and having a limited number of plans to offer people. Lydia assumed that some of her sense of service came from him—that satisfaction he got from getting the very best for his clients.

He'd worn suits all his life, along with an array of astonishingly bright ties, many of which Lydia had given him when she'd been a child. Now, he worked as a part-time handyman. He was always tinkering with something either at their house or at the B&B. He wore comfortable work jeans or Carhartts, and frequently commented that any day he didn't have to put on a jacket or tie was a good day.

"Good afternoon, Mr. Marsh," Alice said formally before returning to her work in the bathroom.

"Was in town to pick up some paint," Dad said. "Figured I'd come see if my best girl wanted to go have coffee or something."

Lydia rolled her eyes. Her dad was always doing this sort of thing. It was how he'd related to his clients, by taking them out to lunch or coffee.

"Sorry, I'll have to take a raincheck," Lydia said. It was already after two PM. The first of her guests would be arriving soon. Fortunately, the restaurant was only open for breakfast and lunch, and had closed for the day. She would put out a signup sheet tomorrow morning to see if there were any guests who wanted to do a wine tasting in the restaurant Saturday evening.

"You go have coffee," Alice said suddenly. She came out into the room and stood with her hands on her waist, glaring at Lydia. "I can finish this room. And do next door, right?"

Lydia bit her lip. Alice could, probably, finish up everything. Lydia would still have to double-check to make sure everything was set up right. But Alice could clean without any oversight.

"All right," Lydia said.

Alice beamed at her. "See? You don't have to work all the time either."

Lydia smiled and shook her head, not commenting on how that really wasn't true.

Fortunately, she enjoyed her work.

Lydia was surprised when after they reached the first floor that her dad didn't go to her own kitchen but actually headed for the door.

"Aren't you coming?" Dad asked when she stopped in the dead center of the now closed restaurant. "I'm buying," he assured her with a teasing grin.

"Uhmmm," Lydia said. She hadn't left the premises in a day. Maybe two. Okay, perhaps she'd been there for most of the week. Or more.

"You need to get out more," Dad gently chided. "Or are you going to turn into ashes and blow away if you actually step out into the sunlight?"

"Very funny," Lydia said as she followed her dad out of the building. The B&B was located on Main Street, just two blocks from the central intersection that made up what was called downtown by the town of Lake Hope, though it was just a few blocks of occupied buildings, not a proper downtown like a city might have.

Lydia paused for a moment, closing her eyes and taking a

deep breath, feeling the sunlight hit her face. It was warm out here, warmer than she'd expected. She ran the AC in the B&B so it was comfortable, not cold, so she could wear lightweight pants and shoes and not feel sticky or shivery.

Okay. So maybe she could do with some time off and away. She did live in the B&B on the first floor. She had groceries and pastries and everything else delivered. If they needed supplies, Misty generally was the one who went and got them.

While Lydia had spent a little bit of time in the garden behind the building, obviously it wasn't enough.

She opened her eyes and smiled at her dad, who was looking at her with a worried expression.

"I'm fine," she assured him. "Just—I guess needed a break more than I realized."

He gave her a big smile. "Then I have just the ticket." He turned and strolled up the street.

Lydia following, uncertain if she should be worried or pleased.

3

---

*L*ydia always loved how Patrice's bakery smelled—of butter and sugar, almonds and cinnamon—with the scent of rich coffee underneath. Like Lydia, Patrice served sandwiches for lunch, but was open a little bit later in the afternoons, until four PM.

The shop had a long glass counter at the front, stuffed full of cookies, donuts, muffins, and slices of sweet quickbread cakes. Only four tables were inside the shop, with a half dozen outside under colorful patio umbrellas. The AC ran on high here, due to the ovens in the back. Soft music played—a service that Patrice paid for and was forever trying to talk Lydia into as well. However, Lydia wanted her space quiet. She couldn't stand to have noise like that in the background all the time.

Patrice had inherited the bakery from her parents. She'd worked there all her life, running it on her own for the last six years after her father had retired. She'd renamed it to *The Palace Bakery* at that time, as she was certainly the queen of her domain.

Gracie came out of the back, hearing the door chime

when Lydia and her dad came in. She wiped her hands on her apron and gave them a huge grin when she saw them. Gracie had worked in the bakery for the last eight years, starting while she'd been in high school. She had talked more than once of opening up her own sideline of pot pies one day. She endured jokes about volleyball and the weather, as she was over six feet tall, though she wasn't athletic at all. She wore her dark frizzy hair pulled back into a tight bun. Her apron showed stains of flour, as well as what looked like streaks of strawberry jam.

"Just me right now," Gracie said when she saw Lydia. "Patrice will be back later this afternoon. Had to make a cake delivery."

Local wineries hired Patrice to make wedding cakes for them. She didn't do them often, but they were beautiful, fanciful creations that looked amazing, with stained glass sugar effects or more restrained pure white affairs. They just tasted like cake to Lydia, something that she'd never tell her friend, though everyone else raved about them.

"That's all right," Lydia said. "I brought a date."

"What'll you have then, Mr. Marsh?" Gracie asked with a smile.

"Coffee and a molasses cookie for me," he said. "And for you?" he asked, turning to Lydia.

What the hell. "Decaf and a slice of the lemon-lavender olive-oil cake."

"Ooooh," Dad said.

"You get a bite. That's all," Lydia warned.

"Of course!" Dad said, throwing his hands up in mock surrender.

He paid for their treats, gathered them up, then led Lydia to a table outside. She slid her chair so she was out of the sunshine. While it might feel nice after all the AC, she knew she would overheat quickly.

"What are you painting?" Lydia asked after she'd taken a bite of her cake. It was divine, with a lovely sharp lemon taste that paired well with the richness of the olive oil and the lightness of the lavender. They both faced the quiet street. Not many cars would go by at this time of the afternoon. Not much foot traffic either, just a few tourists ambling by and window shopping. More would show up after four, when everyone returned from visiting the nearby wineries.

"Painting?" Dad asked, seemingly confused.

"You'd said that you were coming into town to get some paint," Lydia reminded him.

"Oh! Right. Painting," Dad said. "Uhmmm, I'm not sure." He paused, then shrugged. "I'd actually just come in to talk with you."

A stab of fear went through Lydia.

"What do you mean? What's wrong?"

There was something wrong with her mother. She just knew it. Mom had been moping around the last time Lydia had seen her, two weeks ago? Three?

"No, nothing's wrong," Dad assured her. "We just have some things we wanted to tell you."

"About?" Lydia asked. She took a quick sip of her coffee and scalded her mouth. Great.

Dad sighed as he broke apart a piece of his cookie. The smell of molasses and ginger wafted over to Lydia.

"After your mother retired last year, well, it hasn't gone as she'd expected."

Lydia nodded. Mom had worked as a legal secretary for the one honest law firm in Lake Hope, though there were only two. Though she was older than Dad, she'd waited until she was sixty to retire.

Not just Lydia had been worried about what Helen Marsh would do with herself in retirement. She didn't have many hobbies, and she couldn't garden all day and all night.

She had spent a lot of time sleeping and reading the first month. Then she'd started complaining. As well as moping.

"We've decided to go vacationing for the summer," Dad said. "RVing."

"Are you buying an RV?" Lydia asked, stunned. That seemed so out of character for her stay-at-home parents.

"Nope. Renting. For three months," Dad said. "I wouldn't buy one until after we'd spent a lot of time driving one around, you know?"

"Okay," Lydia said slowly. She felt her heart start to return to normal. Maybe nothing was seriously wrong with her mother. She could work with this.

"So, do you want me to take care of the house while you're gone?" Was this what he'd meant by finding her something that would get her out of the B&B more? That seemed kind of mean, however.

Lydia would miss both of them, though honestly, she'd probably miss her dad more.

"Nope! No need to pile one more thing on your plate," Dad said. He sounded weirdly pleased with himself. "Though I do think it might be good for you to get out of your place more often, I didn't want to burden you. You already work too much."

Lydia rolled her eyes. Seemed that was the theme of the day.

"Your brother is going to stay there for the summer," Dad went on.

"Theo?" Lydia said, incredulous. "But—why? He hates it here. And what about Quentin?"

Her younger brother, Theodore Marsh, had gone to Spokane, WA for college and never looked back. He'd gotten a job as a middle-grade teacher, then gotten married and had a young boy named Quentin.

Then he'd gotten divorced. Lydia didn't know the details,

and didn't want to know. However, as far as Lydia was concerned, the first signs she'd ever seen of her younger brother becoming an adult was how he'd handled his life after the divorce. He'd stayed in Spokane, even stayed friendly with his spouse, for the sake of their child.

"Jasmine and Quentin are going to be spending the summer in Mexico, visiting her family," Dad said. "And Theo wanted to come home for a while."

"Really?" Lydia asked, still confused. "Why would he want to do that?"

Dad shrugged. "He just said he needed to get out of Spokane. He was the one who had asked about coming home for a couple of weeks, before we'd finalized the plans with the RV."

"Huh," Lydia said. Her younger brother was coming back to town. That had to be better than Mom being sick. Right?

"So I expect you to spend some time with him," Dad said, giving Lydia a *look*.

Lydia didn't whine and immediately ask, "Do I have to?" though a part of her wanted to. She recognized that was just an old habit from when she'd been much younger and had been told that it was her responsibility to look after her stupid little brother.

But honestly, she'd never gotten along with him, even after they'd become adults. His life was so radically different than hers. He'd grown more conservative, less open, as he'd gotten older. They had practically nothing in common anymore.

Still, Lydia would do anything for her parents. "Of course I'll spend time with him," she assured Dad.

"I want you to put reminders into your calendar to go and talk with him," Dad instructed. "Otherwise, you'll never even leave that building of yours."

Lydia sighed and pulled out her phone. Dad was right. She wouldn't necessarily even remember that Theo was in town until the end of the summer.

It was just one more thing to do.

Dad told her the dates. Theo would be arriving that afternoon. Her parents were taking off that Monday.

Of course they were. That was how her family worked. You arranged everything ahead of time and then just did it. It had driven Neil, her ex-husband, crazy. He'd wanted to be more involved with the planning stages, but he'd never been able to make a decision, not like Lydia. Which was why it had been such a shock to her when he'd presented her with the divorce papers, everything already set into place.

"I'll miss you," Lydia told her dad after they finished their treats and coffee.

"No, you won't," Dad said with a smile. "You'll be working all summer and won't even notice."

Lydia sighed. He might be right. Then again, he might not be. She drew a lot of strength and comfort from knowing her parents were nearby.

"You'll be fine," he added, squeezing her shoulder and kissing her cheek. "And besides, you'll still have family in town. Your brother will be here!"

Lydia didn't think that would make it any better. Still, she agreed to go have coffee with Theo Monday afternoon, and possibly dinner as well.

Maybe they could make a habit of meeting every Monday night. That would at least give her an excuse to leave the B&B once a week.

She told herself that it was all going to be fine with her brother here for the summer. Really, what could go wrong?

4

———

"So, it seems our poltergeist is back," Misty announced as she came into the kitchen Saturday morning.

Lydia looked up from the cantaloupe she was carefully slicing. The kitchen smelled of sweet melon and grapes, part of the fruit salad she was serving with breakfast. Lydia had already eaten, having learned early that if she didn't eat before she made food she'd be miserable.

The cost of a night's stay at the B&B included pastries from Patrice's shop, juice or fruit salad, and coffee or tea for breakfast. For a little bit more, the guests could have eggs, bacon, and pancakes as well. Most people splurged on the extras. They were on vacation, after all.

The grill behind Lydia was still warming up as she sliced fruit, layering the air with the familiar scent of cooking oil. She'd start cooking bacon once it had heated all the way.

"So what did the poltergeist do this time?" Lydia asked as she continued slicing. Of course the B&B was haunted, or at least that was what she told guests. It was good for business, gave them more stories to tell. More than one tourist had sworn they'd seen a ghost on the second floor. Lydia always listened to their stories with interest, though she didn't believe a single one of them.

Ghosts just didn't fit into her practical world view.

"Moved one of the pens into the holder with the letter openers," Misty said. She leaned one hip against the doorway, making herself comfortable. "And also switched around some of the glasses, putting them on the shelves with the mugs, and vice versa."

They didn't really have a poltergeist. What they did have was a local who went into the shop and moved things around. It had taken Misty a while to realize that the moved items served as a distraction, so that no one would notice anything missing.

"Did they take anything this time?" Lydia asked. She finished with the melon she was working on and reached for the next cantaloupe, carefully slicing it in two, the guts of it spilling out over her cutting board.

"I'm not sure, not until I do inventory next week, but I think one of the letter openers is missing," Misty said with a frown. "One of the pretty ones, with the purple agate handle."

Lydia sighed. Whoever it was didn't take things every week. They just moved them around. They seemed to be able to vaguely control themselves most of the time, and only stole something once every six weeks or so.

As their "poltergeist" had only started visiting the gift shop after the first of the year, both Lydia and Misty had a pretty good idea of who it was.

Schooner Thomas.

"Why is that man stealing knickknacks?" Lydia asked, frustrated as she scooped out melon seeds. "What is he doing with them?"

"I think it's a spell," Misty said firmly.

Lydia rolled her eyes.

"I'm serious! I think he's some kind of witch and is trying to put a hex on you," Misty said.

"Are there male witches? Or would he be a warlock instead?" Lydia mused.

"I don't know," Misty said. "But mark my words. He isn't up to any good."

Lydia blinked, surprised. She hadn't ever heard Misty say anything bad about anyone. "What did Schooner do to get on your bad side?" Lydia asked after a moment.

"Ack. It doesn't matter what he said to me," Misty said. "But he was mean to Alice, and I won't stand for that."

"He what?" Lydia asked, putting down the knife carefully before she marched right out and stabbed someone.

"Was mean to her," Misty said, sniffing once with disdain, pushing off with her hip and standing up straight. "I didn't think Alice would say anything to you. But I had the impression it wasn't the first time. I only found out about it because I came walking in and heard him."

Lydia felt her temperature rise, and it had nothing to do with the grill behind her. She could just imagine what sort of impolite things someone like Schooner Thomas might say to a developmentally disabled young woman.

"He's no longer welcome here," Lydia said with finality.

"Good," Misty said with a nod. "You tell him that when he comes in. I'll back you up."

Lydia smirked at her.

"What?" Misty asked, sounding offended.

"There's a Mama Bear underneath all that kindness and love," Lydia teased.

"You're darned tootin'," Misty said in a huff. "And them claws and teeth are sharp."

Lydia was still giggling as she went back to chopping, glad that she finally had an excuse for kicking Schooner

Thomas out of her establishment. It said right there on the door that she could refuse service to anyone. And she'd had enough of his sourness spoiling her service.

However, Schooner Thomas didn't come in that Saturday. Or Sunday.

And Monday afternoon, Alice came to work with the news that Schooner Thomas was dead.

5

"What do you mean, he's dead?" Lydia asked, astonished. She stood in the laundry room with a clean sheet in her hands, unable to process or to keep folding. The machines were quiet behind her. She'd finished serving breakfast early that morning, and had pulled the dirty linens out of all the rooms and washed them already. It felt good to be so far ahead, particularly on a Monday, after a fairly busy weekend with all the rooms occupied.

"He's dead," Alice said with satisfaction. She stood nodding her head at Lydia, as if it were the most normal thing in the world for Schooner Thomas to have died. She wore a navy blue shirt and jeans. Shouldn't she be wearing black if she was carrying such news?

"Who told you that Schooner was dead?" Lydia said. How did Alice know about it? Would her parents tell her? But why?

"Here," Alice said. She took the sheet from Lydia's still unmoving hands and started to fold it. "Mitch told me."

That made even less sense. Lydia wondered if this was part of the novel that Mitch was writing. Sometimes Alice confused fictional stories that she'd been told with true, real things.

"Why does Mitch think that Schooner Thomas is dead?" Lydia said, reaching for one of the clean pillowcases in the dryer and starting to fold that automatically. It warmed her hands, which had suddenly grown cold.

"He heard it on his scanner," Alice said solemnly as she finished folding the sheet.

"What scanner?" Lydia asked. "Like a police scanner?"

Alice gave her a great smile. "Yes! It's a scanner the police use to catch bad people."

That made a little more sense. "Why does Mitch have a police scanner?"

"It's for his novel," Alice said, obviously tired of having to explain even the simplest things. "It's *research*."

The way Alice stressed that word made Lydia wonder what else Mitch had bought or had done all in the name of that holiest of quests: book research.

"I wouldn't go around telling everyone that Schooner Thomas is dead," Lydia said slowly as she reached for a warm towel. "Not until we hear from a more official source. Like the police or on the news or something."

"But I didn't like him," Alice complained.

"I know," Lydia said. "I didn't like him either. And he can't come here anymore. But until I hear from someone other than Mitch and his scanner, I wouldn't necessarily believe that Schooner is dead. Not yet, anyway."

Alice pouted at her. "But why?"

"It might not be true," Lydia said. "And we don't want to be spreading lies, right? What would happen if he walked in here tomorrow? Though I wouldn't let him stay."

Alice sighed. "I'd be sad."

"I would be too," Lydia admitted honestly. "But maybe

the police were wrong. Maybe he wasn't really dead. Maybe a doctor can save him."

There wasn't an adequate hospital nearby—closest one was in Yakima, which was a good two-hour drive away.

"Mitch said he was dead," Alice said, sticking to her story.

"But Mitch only heard it. He didn't see it for himself," Lydia said.

Alice looked stubborn for a moment, before she nodded. "But he was going to go see. After he dropped me off. I told him he could just walk to the house. But Mitch didn't want to. He wanted to drive by and get a feel for the area."

"Walk to Schooner Thomas's house?" Lydia asked, surprised. "Have you ever done that?"

Alice grabbed another sheet from the dryer and started folding it. "Maybe. But you can't tell!" she said, suddenly looking up. "Please!"

"What were you doing at Schooner Thomas's house?" Lydia said as she got another towel to fold, needing the warmth on her hands again.

"Throwing eggs," Alice said slyly. "Not any of the good ones," she assured Lydia. "Just the rotten ones."

Lydia tried not to laugh or encourage the young woman to continue such behavior. Still, she was pleased to know that Alice could, it seemed, take care of herself. "And when did you go throw eggs at Schooner's house?"

Alice thought for a moment, counting back in her head. "Friday night?" she guessed. She shrugged. "I don't know."

"Okay," Lydia said. She took the last towel from the dryer. "You know that you're not supposed to do that sort of thing, right?"

Alice nodded. "But no one is supposed to call me names, either," she said. "Not like he did."

Lydia didn't have to ask what names Schooner had used.

She could guess. "Well, if he isn't dead, and he ever does something like that again, you need to tell me. Promise?"

"But he's dead!" Alice insisted.

Lydia sighed. "We'll see," she said as she gathered up the clean linens. "Let's go get some rooms clean, all right?"

"Okay!" Alice said cheerfully.

Lydia glanced into the dining room on her way up the stairs. There weren't too many people there. Mondays tended to be their least busy lunch. But she'd still set Alice to cleaning the rooms upstairs and come back down to see if Misty needed any help.

And maybe to see if anyone else had heard the news.

6

———

*L*ydia texted Patrice a vague message, merely asking her if she'd heard anything, and to ignore the text if she hadn't. Patrice replied with an emoji—a smiley face scratching her head in confusion, so Lydia assumed that Patrice hadn't heard anything either.

It wasn't until Jen McGowen, Alice's mother, came to pick up her daughter that Lydia got any further news.

Jen was prematurely gray, or at least that was what she claimed. None of the black remained in her hair, which she wore in a short, masculine style that suited her. Lydia could see Alice's features in her mother's face, the rounded cheeks and smiling blue eyes. Jen always wore comfortable farm clothing, heavy jeans even during the heat of the summer, with loose brown or navy blue T-shirts that hid her muscles. She was short as well, maybe five-four, but came across as a powerhouse.

"So, my sister's youngest boy, Mitch, is here visiting," Jen said. "He'll be here for the next few weeks. You should come over sometime."

"It's tourist season," Lydia explained, hoping that would

be enough of an excuse. "But I did hear some news this morning. From Alice. About Schooner Thomas."

Jen looked over at her daughter. "We talked about this," she said sternly.

Alice returned the stern look, though with an added dose of stubborn. "I don't like that man," she stated plainly.

Jen sighed. This wasn't the hill she wanted to die on, obviously. "Mitch went by the house after he dropped you off," she said slowly. "Sergeant Gonzales was there, and there was police tape across the door."

"See! Mitch said he was dead," Alice said.

Lydia blinked, surprised. She hadn't expected that at all. Why hadn't anyone come by with the news? In a close community like Lake Hope, she would have expected everyone to be commenting about such an occurrence.

However, Lydia couldn't ask Jen if she thought Schooner was dead. It was obvious that Jen didn't want to talk about it in front of Alice.

"I'm sure we'll learn all about it later," Lydia said.

"We should go see what Papa's gotten up to this afternoon," Jen told Alice, putting her arm over her daughter's shoulder and leading her out of the B&B.

Lydia smiled. The McGowen's really were the nicest people. Even if they were still trying to set her up with Mitch. She turned and headed back toward the kitchen, to make sure that everything was ready for tomorrow's breakfast. Misty had gone to fetch supplies for the morning, so she was alone in the B&B.

Before she could get started with anything, the door leading to the outside opened and the bell tinkled merrily.

None of the guests coming in that evening had told her about an early check-in. She was sure of it. Must be some tourists looking for…something.

Lydia put on her best smile and walked back out into the

restaurant. "I'm sorry, the restaurant is closed for the afternoon," she told the young man waiting there. She'd turned off the lights and everything, hoping to discourage people from coming in.

He gave her an aggravated sigh. "You forgot, didn't you?" he asked.

Lydia blinked. Her world shook apart, then righting itself again, and she recognized the person in front of her.

"I didn't forget," Lydia lied staring at her little brother Theodore. It didn't matter that he was at least half a head taller than she was. She would always think of him as her little brother.

Theo had grown…thinner, she guessed was probably the best way to describe it. He felt like a shadow to her, as if the last few years had worn him down from the inside. He had the same petite Marsh nose that she did, though his had grown sharper with age. He wore his dark brown hair short enough that the front of it stood up stiffly from his broad forehead, like a teen-idol wannabe, making his oval face seem even longer. His eyes looked hooded and dark, carrying secrets and pain. He wore an off-white shirt with the sleeves rolled up, showing off pasty white forearms with no muscle tone, as well as khaki shorts and black sandals.

Ed and Alan would have been appalled at Theo's lack of fashion sense. The only good thing she could say was that at least Theo wasn't wearing socks with his sandals, though she would bet that come fall when it was cooler, he would.

"How are you?" Lydia asked quietly, as if talking to a horse who might spook and run off.

Lydia had gone to see her parents on Sunday night to say goodbye. However, Theo had been out, so she hadn't seen him.

"Fine," Theo said. He seemed angry. But he still asked, "How are you?"

Lydia smiled at him. "About the same. Busy."

Theo looked around the empty room. "I can tell," he said, the sarcasm dripping from his words.

Lydia thought about taking offense. She knew that his words would have automatically set up the back of her younger self. However, she *was* busy most of the time. And she actually did have her life mostly together, the lack of a partner being her only pain point. She had good friends, a good business, and generally enjoyed herself.

While it would have been nice to become friends with her brother, she didn't need it. And she really didn't need his sourness in her life.

"Misty has stepped out for a minute—do you remember her?" Lydia said, leading Theo deeper into the restaurant, not bothering to turn on the lights.

Theo shook his head.

"So I'm going to make you the best coffee in town, free of charge!" Lydia continued. "I also have some pastries left over from this morning. Next time, I really will remember and we can go someplace else. Deal?"

"Deal," Theo said, sliding into one of the chairs at the table closest to the back counter.

Lydia pulled out a small French press and poured in the perfect amount of ground beans, then added hot water from the automatic coffee brewer and let the press steep. "Are you hungry? Want anything to nibble?" she asked as she fetched two cups.

"Sure," Theo said.

"Raspberry bizmark?" Lydia asked, remembering that had at one point been his favorite.

"You got one?" Theo said, seemingly impressed for the first time that afternoon.

"Maybe," Lydia said. She went searching in the kitchen and came out triumphant. She didn't like filled donuts herself

—she was all about chocolate croissants, sweet and salty and buttery, which fortunately she couldn't get at Patrice's place, otherwise she might have ballooned up to three times her current weight.

She got a ginger molasses cookie for herself and put a few other goodies in a nice arrangement on a plate before coming back out.

"You always have to have things just so," Theo said, his tone complaining even as he eagerly reached for his bizmark.

"What do you mean?" Lydia asked.

Theo indicated the table. "Everything's arranged perfectly," he accused her. "Even if you didn't remember I was coming."

"I like things to look nice," Lydia said. And she did. It was something else Ed and Alan had taught her, about how to make everyday art, as they called it.

She wasn't a great painter or interior designer. Her graphical art skills were laughable. As was her handwriting—Misty wrote up all the price tags and information cards about the items in the gift shop.

However, Lydia could still make art out of everyday things, like making sure that the plates she sent out of the kitchen looked appetizing and that everything was always clean and tidy.

"Why are you back, Theo?" Lydia said after she pushed down the plunger and served them both coffee in mugs that yes, she had set out with matching saucers and little coffee spoons. She'd done a complete service without even thinking about it.

"Mom and Dad needed me to look after their place," Theo said. He added three heaping spoonfuls of sugar to his coffee before he'd even tasted it.

"Dad said you were planning on coming here before he'd told you about their grand adventure," Lydia said. She took her own coffee black, like Dad did. And while it wasn't the best coffee around, she didn't serve cheap stuff either.

It had always been her policy to serve her guests only food that she, herself, would eat. Which meant real eggs, not powdered. Real bacon as well. The pancakes came from a box, but it was a good one. And the coffee was very drinkable, from a localish roaster.

"I needed…I needed to sort some things out," Theo said.

"Like what?" Lydia asked.

Theo shrugged and took a sip of his coffee. "Things," he said distinctly, effectively ending the conversation.

"Fine," Lydia said. "Be that way." She sipped her own coffee, sitting quietly for a few moments with her brother.

It was odd, him being here. What did he need to do back in the town they'd both grown up in? It wasn't merely to sort *things* out. Something else was going on. Call it sister's intuition. It wasn't as though they'd been hanging out recently. The last time she'd seen him had been eighteen months ago—Christmas before last—when he'd brought Quentin home for a few days, without Jasmine.

The bell over the door rang again. Lydia looked up, hoping that it was Misty returned with something that Lydia would have to do right away, anything to give her an excuse to not have to sit and stew with her brother.

But it was Patrice, instead. "Have you heard the news?" she asked, sounding breathless as she came in, as if she'd just run from her shop three blocks away. "Oh." She came to an abrupt halt. "It's you," she added, addressing Theo. She sounded tentative, as if she wasn't sure what her reception to this party was going to be.

Lydia looked between her brother and her best friend, pinging back and forth. Patrice looked as beautiful as she always did. Her frizzy golden hair threatened to escape the bun she'd carefully created that morning, giving her a shining halo. She wore just the slightest amount of makeup to enhance her natural beauty—a touch of mascara, eye liner around her brilliant blue eyes, her lips slightly reddened. Patrice always looked as though she was about to tear off her apron and go to some fabulous party. Lydia usually felt shlumpy in comparison.

"You didn't tell me that he was coming to town," Patrice accused Lydia.

"Didn't know I was supposed to," Lydia said. She wasn't about to admit out loud that she'd forgotten.

"Hello, Patrice," Theo said. He had plastered a nice enough smile across his face. Dad would be proud. "What news? As someone obviously forgot to mention me," he said, throwing a sneer Lydia's way.

"About Schooner Thomas!" Patrice said. "He's dead!"

"What?" Theo said, suddenly standing. "How? Why? What happened?"

"Don't know the details yet," Patrice said as she reached across the counter and snagged herself a mug. "This was what you meant by your text earlier, wasn't it?" she asked Lydia as she sat down and poured herself some coffee.

"Alice said that her cousin Mitch had heard the news on his police scanner," Lydia admitted.

"And you didn't tell me?" Theo said, glaring at Lydia as he sat back down again.

"I didn't know for certain if it was true or not," Lydia said, shrugging. "And I didn't want to spread a false rumor. What did you hear?" she asked Patrice.

"Well, you know Becky St. John, who lives two doors down from Schooner? She said the police have been going in and out of the house all day. Then the ambulance came and they carried away a body wrapped in a sheet. No one knows what's going on. The police won't say anything."

"They can't," Theo said.

"Why not? They should at least tell the neighbors so they know what's going on," Patrice grumbled.

"They have to notify next of kin before they make a general announcement," Theo said.

"Oh, that makes sense," Patrice said. She took a big bite out of one of the cookies Lydia had set out and then sighed heavily.

"You haven't eaten all day, right?" Lydia asked pointedly.

"Maybe?" Patrice admitted. "I just got so busy this morning."

"Should I make you a sandwich?" Lydia said.

"No, I'll be fine. I have a nice Portobello steak waiting for me at home," Patrice said.

That was something else that differentiated the pair of them. Patrice was a hard-core vegetarian, had been one for the longest time, while Lydia liked her steak and meatloaf and hot dogs and lamb roasts and anything else she could afford.

"Who do you think killed him?" Patrice asked.

"Why do you think someone killed old Schooner?" Lydia asked. "Maybe he died of a heart attack or something."

"Oh, please," Theo said. "Nobody liked him. I bet somebody grew tired of his nastiness and knifed him. About time, too."

"What did Schooner Thomas do to you?" Lydia said, surprised at her brother's vehemence.

"Nothing," he said, shooting a look at Patrice.

There was some sort of story going on between the pair of them, and neither had thought to include her, Lydia was certain of it.

"Fine. Keep you secrets," Lydia said. She had a few of her own that she wasn't about to share.

The three of them sat in the dimly lit restaurant, remembering old hurts.

"Theo's going to be here for the next few months," Lydia finally said after a few more cold moments, trying to bring them all back into the warmth. "While my parents are out having adventures." They'd promised to call regularly, as well as send postcards of all the fabulous sights they were visiting.

"Ah," was all the response Patrice gave. "Well, I should be going back to the shop. Text me later, okay?" she said as she stood to leave.

Misty came in just then. Patrice slipped out as Lydia introduced Theo to Misty (who remembered him) and then he was gone as well.

"What was all that about?" Misty asked as she helped Lydia clear the table they'd been using, carrying everything back into the brightly lit kitchen.

"I have no idea," Lydia said. "And quite frankly, I'm not sure I want to know."

"Course you do," Misty said. "You're as curious as I am."

The bell to the door tinkled, and Misty went to see greet their first guests for the evening.

Lydia put away the bread, fresh fruit, and juice into the walk-in while she thought about the strange currents that had flowed between Patrice and Theo. And what Theo had against Schooner. Had the old man just died? Or had he been killed?

Whatever was going on, Lydia was certain that while she might be curious, she would probably be better off not knowing.

7

Sergeant Alex Gonzales walked into the *Nip & Bud* Tuesday just after the lunch rush had finished. He'd scared Lydia as a girl, glowering at her and the other kids anytime he came to visit the school, back when he'd just been a deputy. He wasn't very tall, and had a barrel chest which gave him a surprisingly deep voice for his size. His black hair was starting to gray a little along the temples and sideburns, making him look even meaner. He had dark skin and three small moles under his chin, like an old-fashioned witch, someone who would eat children. His forehead was perpetually creased, making it look as though he was always scowling even when he smiled.

Dad had always gotten along well with him, but then again, her dad got along with everyone.

"Can I help you officer?" Lydia asked as she put the dish bucket back down on the table she'd been clearing and wiped her hands off on her apron.

The sergeant didn't eat at Lydia's restaurant often. The two officers who shared all the policing duties for Lake Hope tended to eat lunch at The Cove, which was just up the street, and was more of a bar than a restaurant. Fortunately, she'd never had to call the police, though she'd threatened a few times when dealing with overly drunk tourists.

"Lydia Marsh?" Sergeant Gonzales asked, squinting at her with his dark eyes.

"Yes," Lydia said. Who else would she be? He surely knew her on sight, right? "What can I do for you?" She wasn't in trouble with the law, as far as she knew. Crap. Had something happened to her parents? They'd been killed in an accident and the officer had come to warn her. Her heart suddenly beat loudly and her throat dried out.

"We'd like you to come down to the station at your convenience," Sergeant Gonzales said, making it sound as though it had better be convenient for her right now.

That…didn't sound as if it was her parents. He'd tell her here and now, right? Lydia made herself take a deep breath, pulling herself back from that bleak edge.

"What do you want to see me about?" Lydia said as she started untying her apron, hoping the sergeant didn't notice her shaking hands.

"I'll explain once we reach the station," the sergeant said.

"I need to let Misty know that I'm going," Lydia said, picking up the dish bucket and walking back into the kitchen, unsurprised that the sergeant followed her.

"Ah, *hola*!" Misty said as Sergeant Gonzales came into the room. "*¿Cómo estás?*"

Lydia had learned Spanish in high school, as had most everyone else. Though she was not fluent in it, Misty was, which was handy around here.

"*Buenas tardes, señora*," the sergeant said to Misty, nodding. "I need to speak with Ms. Marsh down at the station for a bit."

That earned him a huge smile, which surprised Lydia.

"Good, good," Misty said. "I'll hold down the fort here," she assured Lydia.

"Thank you," Sergeant Gonzales said with a nod of his head to Misty. "Shall we go?" he said, turning to Lydia, growing more formal.

Of course, Sergeant Gonzales was friendly with Misty. She liked everyone, and everyone liked her. It didn't matter that Lydia had also been born and raised in Lake Hope. People just gravitated toward Misty.

Lydia put on her best smile and led the sergeant out of the B&B.

As always, it was much warmer outside than Lydia expected. She was glad that she had on shorts that day that went down to her knees, with colorful red and white hibiscus flowers on them, making her feel pretty. She also had on brown canvas sneakers and an off-white T-shirt which the apron had managed to spare from the usual stains. Her hair was braided and her bobby pins held back any wisps, keeping it out of her eyes while she worked. Ed and Alan would probably have given her a B for effort, but downgraded her on chicness.

The sun shone down brightly from a pale blue sky, the asphalt reflecting it back in waves of sheen, making it seem like the heat of summer was already upon them. The smell of tar rose from the street, thick and sticky. The sidewalks had been redone recently, with small squares of concrete instead of larger blocks, an artistic look that was a pain to keep up. When the chamber of commerce had proposed the new sidewalks, Lydia had voted against it. She'd been right— while the smaller blocks gave the area a more historic feel, she now had a constant battle with grass and weeds growing in the cracks, at least until the heat of the summer when everything died back.

The police station was only a block and a half away, just

off Main Street, in a newer building. Lydia was old enough to remember the old warehouse that had been there when she was a kid.

"Is this about Schooner Thomas?" Lydia asked as they walked down the street. They passed three people she knew as they made their way along the sidewalk. She could just imagine the rumors that were already being put into the mill.

"I'd rather wait to talk about it until we reached the station," Sergeant Gonzales said.

They walked in frosty silence for a few moments before the sergeant asked, "How is your father?"

"He and Mom went on a trip for the summer," Lydia said. "They're out RVing for the next few months."

"Really?" Sergeant Gonzales said. "Huh."

"I know, right?" Lydia said. "I had never expected them to just take off like that."

A thoughtful look crossed the sergeant's face. "When did they leave?"

"Monday morning," Lydia said.

"Hmmm," the sergeant replied. "Are you taking care of their place?"

"No, my brother, Theodore, is. He's here for the summer."

"And when did he arrive?"

Lydia wasn't sure if there was something behind all the questions or if he was just being nosy. "Friday, I think. I didn't see him until yesterday."

She still wasn't sure what Theo was doing in Lake Hope either. Or what was going on between him and Patrice.

For a small town—practically a village—there was suddenly so much going on!

The Sergeant stepped in front of Lydia and opened the door to the station for her. There was a small counter running across the front of the room, with two desks behind it, for the two officers, Sergeant Gonzales and Deputy Virginia Markus, who wasn't there at the time. The room was done in shades of government beige and smelled of stale coffee. The only personal touches that Lydia saw were a bright-blue plush hedgehog on one desk, and two small framed photos on the other desk. Everything else felt as though it had been issued by the state, along with instructions for how it should be displayed, like the American flag, the Washington state flag, and the (ugh) picture of the state governor with his smarmy smile.

"Come with me," the sergeant said. He lifted up part of the counter so Lydia could walk past it, then led her along a small hallway that went down the center of the station. More photos hung here, showing the officers happy and smiling, posing with members of the community. The Sergeant opened up a door on the right to a small room.

An interrogation room, Lydia would bet, having seen enough cop shows on TV. There was a one-way glass mirror on the right wall, a small white table directly in front of her, and two chairs. The place felt cold and sterile, despite the worn brown carpet that gave off a musty smell. A pile of folders sat on one side of the table, so Lydia sat on the other side, facing the mirror.

It was only after she'd sat down that she realized she'd been subtly maneuvered to sit in that seat. Was Deputy Markus watching her from behind the mirror? Lydia shifted uncomfortably on the chair, feeling as though she was a kid again and had been brought in front of the principal, though she'd never gotten into that much trouble when she'd been in school.

At least, nothing that anyone ever learned about.

"Can I get you anything? Water? Coffee?" the sergeant asked after she'd sat down.

"No, nothing," Lydia said. She didn't want to ask for

something and then have him disappear on her for hours, like cops did on shows. She had work to do.

"Okay." The Sergeant smiled at her again. It looked forced.

He dropped down into the chair facing her and pushed the folders to the side. "Now, what I'm about to tell you is confidential, at least for a bit longer. But Schooner Thomas is dead."

"Really?" Lydia asked. She knew she was going to hell for the wave of relief that went through her at the news. "I mean, I'd heard rumors, of course. It's a small town."

"We've notified Mr. Thomas's ex-wife about his death. But we're still trying to get in touch with his son, Bernard. Once we notify him, we'll make a formal announcement about the death," Sergeant Gonzales said.

That was what Theo had said—that the police wouldn't tell everyone about Schooner's death until after they'd notified the family.

When the sergeant didn't say anything more, Lydia asked, "How did he die?"

"We still don't have the exact cause of death, and we only have an approximate time. So we really haven't been able to build an accurate timeline yet," the sergeant admitted. "But we are treating this like a homicide. There were enough questionable things at the house."

"A murder? Here? In Lake Hope?" Lydia said, stunned. "I just—wow. I never would have imagined it. Here of all places!" That sort of thing happened in places like Seattle or Spokane.

The Sergeant studied her hard for another moment, then his expression softened into something that looked much more genuinely friendly. "I know, right? You grew up here. The last murder we had was four years ago."

Lydia nodded. "Old man Green. Shot his wife."

"And then marched right down here to the station to tell us about it," Sergeant Gonzales said. "Now, you wouldn't have anything to confess, would you?" he said, maintaining a much more easy demeanor—he actually sounded as if he was teasing her.

"Me?" Lydia said, startled. "No. I didn't like Schooner Thomas. But nobody did."

The Sergeant sighed. "And that's the problem. Schooner Thomas didn't have many friends."

Lydia silently amended that to *any* friends. He was sour and a grump and mean to everyone.

The Sergeant opened up the top folder from the stack on his right, then pulled out a page and pushed it to her. "Do you recognize that?"

"Obviously," Lydia said. She just barely managed to hold back her eye roll. "That's one of the letter openers that we sell at the gift shop."

The paper held a printout of a series of pictures of the letter opener, with a ruler next to it to show scale. The opener itself was plain metal on the business side, silver, with blunt edges and tip. The handle was encased in pretty purple agate, with the words, "Nip and Bud, Lake Hope" embossed on one side in golden letters. Lydia thought it was one of the better mementos that they sold.

"Did you ever sell one of these to Schooner Thomas?" the sergeant asked as he put the sheet of paper back into the file folder.

"No," Lydia said. "But Misty and I suspect that he's been stealing things from my shop for the past six months."

"That's a serious allegation," Sergeant Gonzales said. "Tell me about it."

Lydia shrugged. "We couldn't prove it. Otherwise I

would have come to you. But we've only been missing items from the gift shop since the start of the year, when Schooner started coming into my restaurant regularly."

Though if Lydia were being honest with herself, she probably wouldn't have said anything to the police if she had been certain it was Schooner. All she would have done would be to have a quiet word with the other shopkeepers downtown to keep an eye out for Schooner and his light fingers.

"I see," the sergeant said, nodding. "Where were you Friday night?"

Lydia's heart suddenly started pounding again. The police didn't suspect her, did they? She wiped her hands off on her cute shorts, wishing suddenly that she were more covered up.

"I was at an impromptu wine tasting," Lydia said, "that I held in the restaurant."

As she'd started to poll guests about having a wine tasting on Saturday night, she'd discovered that the majority had wanted one on Friday instead. She'd quickly arranged for Elmer from one of the nearby vineyards to come in, bringing a large variety of wines for her guests to taste.

"And after that?" the sergeant asked.

Lydia couldn't help her snort of derision. "I was in bed. Asleep. I had to get up at six the next morning to start breakfast."

Sergeant Gonzales sighed. He peered intently at her, studying her, seeking the truth.

Lydia stared back defiantly. She hadn't done anything wrong! "Am I a suspect?"

The Sergeant sat back in his chair. "Everyone's a suspect at this point," he admitted. "Though I'd like to clear you."

"Was Schooner Thomas killed with that letter opener?" Lydia couldn't help but ask.

"We don't believe so, no. We think he was stabbed with it post mortem."

"Why would someone do that?" Lydia said, confused. "The point is really dull." Or was someone just that angry at Schooner that they wanted to stab him after they'd killed him? That sent a shiver of cold down her spine.

"Do you have any enemies in town that we should know about?" Sergeant Gonzales suddenly asked.

"I don't think so?" Lydia said. "What, do you think someone was trying to frame me?"

"Or throw suspicion your way," the sergeant said, nodding.

Lydia felt another wave of shock wash over her. Who would do such a thing? Though everyone was friendlier with Misty than with her, that didn't meant that anyone actually hated her. Did it?

"Unofficially, I'm going to clear you," Sergeant Gonzales announced. "You haven't been officially cleared yet, not until we get a better timeline."

"Thank you?" Lydia said, surprised. Why would the sergeant clear her like that? Did he have somebody else in mind for the killer?

Or maybe this was some twisted game, and he was going to keep a very careful eye on her, giving her space and time to implicate herself?

She nearly snorted out loud again. This wasn't some sort of misdirection. Sergeant Gonzales was merely smart, not some sort of super genius detective like she saw on TV.

The Sergeant leaned forward against the table again. "We're a small department. It's just me and Deputy Markus," he said, his voice taking on a confidential tone. "We don't have any detectives on staff. We're used to dealing with drunken tourists, not murderers. So we're borrowing a detective from Yakima to help us with this case."

The look of relief on the sergeant's face was almost comical.

"That's good," Lydia said, though she still felt uncomfortable with the entire thing. Who would have killed Schooner Thomas? Was there really someone that angry in town? And why implicate her?

"So the department would like to engage one of your rooms for the next two weeks," Sergeant Gonzales said, returning to business.

Lydia opened her mouth to say no, it was tourist season, she was booked solid. Then she closed it again.

She actually wasn't booked solid, not really. She had at least one open room every day for the next couple of weeks. Starting the fourth of July, she was completely booked until September, but for now, she could, in fact, fit someone in.

"All right," Lydia said slowly. "If it's only for a couple of weeks."

"Probably won't even be that long," the sergeant assured her. "Just that these detectives like to see the crime scene themselves. As if we can't photograph it well enough for them." Sergeant Gonzales indulged himself with his own eyeroll. "But we're grateful for the help," he added quickly. "He's on a per diem from his department, so he'll pay you directly."

"When does he arrive?" Lydia asked. She'd place him in the Marigold room. It was on the third floor and one of her favorites, the walls painted in a delicate shade of yellow with lovely, burnt-orange colored duvet covers. It also had its own ensuite, which she assumed the detective would need.

"He's already here," Sergeant Gonzales said. "He's at the crime scene with Deputy Markus. He'll check into your establishment later this afternoon."

"I see," Lydia said. Had the police department arranged for the detective to stay somewhere else, and had those accommodations fallen though? Or had someone else that the sergeant had "cleared" of the murder suddenly proven untrustworthy?

"Now, remember, we don't want everyone in town to know about Schooner's death," the sergeant said. "Not until we make the official announcement."

"They already know," Lydia said. "They watched the ambulance come and saw a body covered in a sheet being taken out of the house."

Sergeant Gonzales nodded sheepishly. "Yeah, that's what we figured. But all they know is that it's a death, not a murder."

"People saw me walking here today with you," Lydia said. "And they'll see that a detective has arrived."

"True," the sergeant said. He sighed. "But I'd really like for Bernard Thomas to hear the word about his father's death from us and not from a random stranger."

"Where is Bernard living these days?" Lydia asked. "I don't think I've seen him since high school."

"In Yakima," Sergeant Gonzales said. "He recently lost his job, isn't at his apartment, and isn't answering his phone. We don't want to just leave a voicemail message about the death of his father. But we haven't been able to locate him."

Had Bernard also been killed? That would be awful. Lydia didn't know much about Bernard, barely remembered him from high school, but if he'd taken after Schooner...

"Are we finished here?" Lydia said when the sergeant seemed to fall into contemplation.

"We are," he said, nodding. He stood up. "Thank you for your time. I'll send you a message when we reach Bernard."

"Good luck," Lydia said as she stood.

"Thank you," Sergeant Gonzales said. "We'll find the killer," he assured her.

Lydia walked slowly back to the B&B, soaking in the heat of the day.

But even that wasn't enough to fully warm her. Not when there was a murderer running around in her small town.

8

———

"So what did he want?" Misty asked, pouncing on Lydia as soon as she walked into the B&B.

It was nearly three, and Lydia still had two rooms to turn over for guests. Fortunately, the Marigold room was already clean. "He wanted to rent a room for a detective who's coming here from Yakima," Lydia said as she walked directly toward the stairs, hoping to discourage Misty.

She should have known better. While Misty was friendly with everyone, that also meant she knew everyone's business, sometimes better than they knew it themselves.

"Ohhh," Misty said as she followed Lydia up the stairs. "That's good. Now, isn't Sergeant Gonzales a handsome man?"

"Are you crazy?" Lydia said. "He's way too old for me. And he's a cop."

She paused when she reached the second floor landing to look back at Misty. The other woman was dressed in a polo shirt, a maroon color that nicely highlighted her dark skin, with a pair of casual tan slacks. Ed and Alan would proclaim that Misty had mastered the art of what looked good on her.

Despite being so short, she always appeared taller, primarily because she wore longer shirts and then didn't tuck them in, so she wasn't cutting herself in half, as it were.

"The Sergeant is recently single and would be good for you," Misty insisted.

"I'm better off alone," Lydia insisted. And she would be. Sergeant Gonzales was far too angry looking all the time. She did not need to deal with that. Particularly not with Theo and his brooding in town.

"Ah well, you can't blame me for trying," Misty said.

Lydia merely rolled her eyes and continued walking up the stairs.

"So have they cleared you as a suspect?" Misty asked.

"*Unofficially* cleared," Lydia said, wanting to emphasize that.

"Even though they found Schooner stabbed with one of our letter openers?" Misty said.

"How did you know that?" Lydia said. She stopped on the landing between the second and third floors and turned to face the other woman.

"I have a cousin who works in the coroner's office, over in Yakima," Misty said with a dismissive wave of her hand.

"Does everyone know about the letter opener?" Lydia asked. She really wasn't looking forward to trying to explain to her guests how someone was stabbed with something from the gift shop.

Then again, people were weird. Would such news really be bad publicity? Or would everyone suddenly want to buy one and would she have to restock?

"No, no. Just family," Misty said.

Lydia shook her head. The Sergeant wasn't going to be able to keep any secrets from the gossips in town. She just hoped that he realized that it wasn't Lydia who was sharing the information.

"They're trying to find Bernard, to tell him the news about his father, before they make an official announcement to the town," Lydia said.

Misty nodded. "He lives in Yakima. Works in a bar. Turned up drunk for work on Friday, so they gave him the weekend off, with no pay. He makes most of his money on the weekends, so not working was actually a punishment."

"I see," Lydia said. It was actually a little frightening how much Misty and probably all of her family already knew about the case.

That would work for her in the long run, right?

Lydia pulled out her phone once she reached the third floor and double-checked the booking app. Yup. Marigold was free tonight. She'd have to rearrange some of the guests next weekend, but she was pretty sure she could accommodate everyone.

"You're putting the detective in here?" Misty said, following Lydia into Marigold. "Good choice."

Lydia nodded, looking around. The room seemed warm and comfy, done in shades of yellow, orange, and brown. The air still carried a faint lemon smell from the natural cleaner she used. The room was directly above Cornflower, in the northeast corner of the building. It would get morning sunlight, but it wouldn't overheat like the rooms sometimes did on the west side.

The layout of the room was the same as in Cornflower: big bed in the center of the room piled high with matching pillows that Ed and Alan would have approved of, flat screen TV hanging from the wall above the armoire, welcome basket on the desk in the other corner. Lydia double-checked the bathroom, making sure that it had towels, soap, and shampoo all set, everything ready to welcome the next guest.

"The detective will be fine here," Misty announced. She

stood in the doorway and gave a nod of approval, like a doting mother watching her child share toys.

"Do you know who the detective is?" Lydia asked, curious.

"No," Misty said, scowling. "Though my sister-in-law's cousin works for the police department in Yakima, he works in drug enforcement, and the detective works in the major-crime unit. So who knows?"

"Well, we will in a short while," Lydia said. It amused her how offended Misty appeared to be, to not know everything going on about the case.

The sound of the bell on the first floor tinkled merrily. "You better go see who that is," Lydia said, "while I finish making the beds up here."

Misty sighed. "Fine. But don't think that you've gotten away without answering all my questions!"

Lydia grinned as Misty tromped down the stairs. There really wasn't much more she would tell the other woman, not until Sergeant Gonzales gave her the go-ahead.

Then again, how much more could Lydia tell Misty about the case that she hadn't already learned from her numerous cousins?

9

———

*L*ydia was coming back down the stairs around five PM, having settled the last guest. A tall young man stood just inside the doorway of the dining room, looking around. Lydia took a good look at him to make sure that she wasn't mistaking her brother as a stranger again.

Nope. This man was only a little taller than she was, not her brother's height. He had a serious face with pink-toned white skin. Blue eyes peered out from under a wide, intelligent brow. His nose was sharp, though his lips were thin and sensuous. He had brown hair that was just starting to have a few speckles of gray, though she would have put him around her age. He wore a light-colored suit with a black and blue striped tie.

"Can I help you?" Lydia asked coming quickly down the rest of the stairs.

"I'm here about a room," the man said.

"I'm sorry, we don't have any vacancies. You could try *The Lodge*. It's on the western side of the lake," Lydia said automatically. *The Lodge* charged three times her rate, and so often had rooms available. And despite what the owner claimed, his rooms were *not* three times better than everyone else's.

"No, no. I think I have a reservation," the man said. "Ellis Avery."

Lydia frowned and walked into the gift store. The counter there doubled as their registration area, so they just had a single cash register. "No, I don't see your name listed," she said, checking the registration book. She reached for her phone to see if there was a reservation on the app that hadn't made it into the book. It didn't happen more than once a year, but mistakes happened.

"Sergeant Gonzales said he'd arranged everything," Ellis said.

"Oh! You're the detective!" Lydia said. "Sergeant Gonzales never told me your name."

Ellis nodded. "So…I do have a room?" he asked, giving her a charming smile.

"You do!" Lydia said.

Why was her heart suddenly pounding again? She'd already been unofficially cleared of the murder. Surely she wasn't nervous because the detective was a police officer? She hadn't done anything wrong!

Or did it have something to do with Ellis Avery's very nice smile?

"You'll be in Marigold," Lydia said, snagging a key from the locked box under the counter.

They took care of the paperwork and payment, with Lydia studiously looking at Ellis's ID. The picture on his driver's license really didn't do him justice—he appeared angry and scowling in it.

"Thank you," Lydia said, returning his cards to him. "You'll be on the third floor. Follow me."

"No elevator?" the detective asked as he started up the stairs behind Lydia.

"There really isn't a place for one," Lydia said. "So I just have to make sure that all my guests realize that the B&B isn't handicap accessible."

"I see," Ellis said. It sounded as if he disapproved.

"If I'd been building a brand new B&B, I would have to make rooms that were accessible," Lydia explained. "As I was taking over an already established business, I didn't have to. But if I ever come into a windfall, I might add another extra room on the ground floor that would be accessible."

Ellis merely grunted.

What, was he not used to walking up stairs? He didn't appear to be out of shape.

Lydia firmly turned her thoughts away from considering exactly what kind of shape Ellis Avery might be in as she led him straight to the Marigold room.

The detective dropped his duffle bag onto the center of the bed and looked around. Didn't he approve?

Lydia went through her usual spiel about the coffee maker, the towels and soap, the TV and the remote.

"We don't come and clean every day," she warned. "Just let me or Misty know if you need more towels or want the sheets changed or something."

The detective nodded. He gave her a soft smile that transformed his face into something much, much nicer. "Thank you," he said. "I know it's tourist season and you're booked up."

"We can make it work," Lydia said. His eyes really were the most amazing color of blue, almost gray here in the dimmer room.

A moment of quiet passed between the pair of them.

"Ah, is there anything else?" Lydia asked as she suddenly realized the danger she might be in with this handsome stranger. She started backing out of the room.

"When's dinner?" he asked as he looked away, opening up his duffle bag.

"We don't serve dinner here," Lydia told him. "There are some very nice restaurants down the block. Like *The Cove*, or *Rusty's Pub*."

In the back of Lydia's head a tiny voice yelled at her that she should offer to make him a sandwich. She firmly smacked that voice with a huge mallet, knowing that she was playing whack-a-mole at this point.

"Oh. Okay. Thanks," Ellis said.

"But we do serve breakfast. It's included in the B&B fee," Lydia said.

"Then I'll see you tomorrow morning."

"Yes," Lydia said, finally getting out of the room and practically racing down the stairs.

She needed to get hold of herself. Now. She was thirty eight. He lived in Yakima. She was not interested in any sort of relationship, let alone a long-distance one.

However, she feared that it was already too late and that her heart wasn't going to listen to any of her practical advice.

10

Wednesday morning, instead of just throwing on a shirt and shorts, Lydia found herself dithering over what she should wear. Should she put on the peach-colored polo shirt with the white shorts? The shirt would show any stains or sweat quickly, but it made her gray eyes stand out nicely. Or should she maybe wear her plum-colored T-shirt? It wouldn't show any stains, but it was a bit tight across her chest.

Damn it! She wasn't a teenager anymore, trying to catch the eye of the high school quarterback. Besides, she had caught Neil's eye, married him, and then been divorced by him. So enough of this!

Lydia finally put on a loose, navy-blue T-shirt with sage green shorts, then pulled her hair back hard, making sure the braid was neat. She found herself hesitating again—she had both plain bobby pins as well as clips that were fancier, with small flowers glued to the tops of them. She slipped the prettier ones into her hair, then took them out again immediately, replacing them with the plain ones. Ed and Alan would have been proud of her for not over-embellishing her look. They'd told her more often than she cared to remember about always looking in the mirror at the last minute and removing one item.

Besides, she was going to work, not to some party.

Lydia paused and looked at herself critically. She had laugh lines around the corners of her mouth and eyes—they'd grow more pronounced as she aged. Her skin didn't have the age spots her parents did, they'd come at some point, but as she spent more time indoors than out, she might be spared them for quite a few more years. She'd always thought her petite nose was her best feature, and still felt that way. If she spent more time in the sun, she'd tan, but for now, she was fairly white. Her skin had a brown tone to it, not the pink of the detective.

After sighing heavily, Lydia took herself to the kitchen to start her day. There wasn't anything she'd change about her looks, despite not being as fashionable as Patrice. She presented exactly as who she was: a hard-working single woman who found joy in her life. It was just too bad if anyone didn't see that or desire it. Their loss.

Misty took orders in the restaurant that morning while Lydia cooked. It gave Misty the opportunity to check out Ellis Avery, as well spread her homey good-natured cheer around the room.

Turned out that Ellis was a man after Lydia's heart—he requested black tea instead of coffee, then only wanted eggs, bacon, and a small serving of fruit salad. Lydia made sure to serve him her special tea, made up of a blend of English Breakfast with dried ginger, which gave it a rich, spicy flavor.

Once the breakfast diners had cleared out, Misty came back into the kitchen to hang out with Lydia while she finished running the dishes through the sanitizer. Misty wore a smug smile which meant she had news. She was dressed that day in an off-white cotton shirt with tiny flowers done in stripes, along with a pair of casual brown slacks.

"So it turns out Detective Avery is recently single," Misty started off with. "It's part of why he was assigned this case—his superiors thought that getting out of Yakima for a while would be good for him."

"And which cousin told you this?" Lydia teased.

"None of them. I just asked the nice detective," Misty said.

"Really? He volunteered all that?" Lydia said, surprised. Ellis had seemed more close-mouthed than that when he'd been talking to her.

"Well, I may have pushed a little, asking whether his wife would be joining him here on the weekend, and why he'd been assigned here," Misty said. She arched an eyebrow at Lydia, as if to say, "See? That's how it's done."

Lydia shook her head. Only Misty could have asked those sorts of questions without offense, something she never seemed to appreciate.

"He'll only be here a short time," Lydia said. "Then Lake Hope can get back to normal."

"We'll see," Misty said. "Things might feel a little different if the killer has been living among us the whole time."

"I know, right?" Lydia said. She couldn't help the shiver she gave. "I want to feel safe in my hometown. Not as though I have to look over my shoulder all the time."

"Yes, but nobody was as hated as Schooner Thomas," Misty pointed out.

"Then why did someone stab him with one of my letter openers?" Lydia asked. That was the really bizarre part of the case, as someone killing Schooner Thomas was almost understandable.

"I don't know," Misty said. "That's the real mystery. But

don't you worry. I believe Detective Avery will uncover the truth quickly."

"I'm glad that you have such faith in the man," Lydia said. Generally, Misty did have a good sense of people, and Lydia had grown to trust it. Though she had her own radar as well, well-honed now by dealing with tourists coming through constantly. She knew which people she would trust with her cash register and those who would rob her blind. Not that they had planned it, just a crime of opportunity.

Misty didn't reply immediately, but appeared to be thinking. "Although, it might be better if he took his time solving it."

"Why?" Lydia said. She knew what Misty was hinting at and wanted all of this conversation over as quickly and painlessly as possible.

"So that you two have the opportunity to get to know each other," Misty said. The unspoken *duh* resounded in the quiet kitchen.

Lydia rolled her eyes. "Just because a handsome stranger has come into town doesn't mean that we're destined to be together."

"You think he's handsome, huh?" Misty said.

"Leave it be," Lydia warned. She would not be teased about this. Not given the way her thoughts kept drifting back to the man.

"Sure thing, boss," Misty said, raising her hands in the classic "I give up" pose. "Guess I don't need to point out the obvious, then."

Before Lydia could ask what she meant, Misty had ducked out of the kitchen. Lydia shook her head and went back to work, focusing on the job and not on whatever ridiculous future her co-worker had cooked up.

Nor to her errant heart.

11

*J*ust before lunch on Wednesday, Sergeant Gonzales texted Lydia to let her know that the police had found Bernard. He didn't give her any more information than that, though Lydia suspected that if she asked Misty, she'd probably get a full and accurate account of where Bernard had been and why the police had had such difficulty getting in touch with him. Misty probably knew more than Sergeant Gonzales.

Less than thirty minutes after Lydia received the text from the sergeant, Misty came bustling into the kitchen to announce that the news had finally been made public, that her sister had heard it on the radio. (Lake Hope wasn't big enough to have its own radio station. However, there was a station that most people in town listened to. It was located on the eastern side of Yakima and had a signal strong enough to get over the hills that separated Lake Hope from the city.)

"It's about time," Lydia said. Though she'd kept her word and hadn't mentioned anything other than the detective coming to stay at the B&B, it had irked her more than she'd care to admit. She'd wanted to talk with Patrice about whoever might have stabbed Schooner. And possibly dish a little about the detective.

More locals came in for lunch that day than usual—in addition to Dennis Solomon and Tracy Stevenson, Lydia saw Rusty Baker who ran the butcher shop, Kim Wang from the nail salon, and Mr. Ohme, who ran the local home and garden supply. Everyone had a theory as to how exactly Schooner Thomas had died, as well as who had killed him.

Though Rusty and Kim strongly believed that the police should have opened up a hotline so that people could call in if they'd seen anyone suspicious in the area, Lydia privately doubted that would be necessary. Everyone in town would be free with their opinions with the sergeant and his deputy, of that Lydia had no doubt.

It wasn't until later that afternoon that Lydia was able to go see Patrice for an extended, therapeutic gossip session. Detective Avery hadn't come back to the B&B for lunch. He'd probably ended up going to *The Cove*, with the other police officers. She didn't take it as a personal slight. Not at all.

The two friends met in the back of Patrice's bakery. Grace was out making deliveries. Patrice was just finishing up mixing dough. She'd already taken the most recent batch of ginger-molasses cookies out of the oven. Lydia had to admit those might be her favorites, particularly when still warm. She was drinking iced decaf coffee that afternoon, and it made a lovely complement to the cookie.

The lights at the back of the bakery were bright, shining off the spotless stainless steel countertops that ran around the edges of the room, as well as the huge island in the center. Lydia always admired how clean Patrice and Grace kept everything. Large industrial mixers sat next to the oversized sink on the far wall, like beasts all set to do their mistress's bidding. The set of stainless steel refrigerator and freezer hummed to themselves in the corner, quietly radiating contentment. The door that led out to the alley was beside them, the lock and the jam reinforced with metal to prevent break-ins.

Though the space wasn't a home kitchen, Lydia had been back here often enough that it felt cozy to her, despite the modern appliances and hard metal edges. Patrice kept a couple of padded folding chairs in the kitchen, just so friends could sit and talk with her while she worked.

"Tell me all the news about the case!" Patrice said as she slid the first batch of quick-bread cakes into the oven. She wore a tan apron to keep her blouse and shorts clean, along with her usual touches of makeup that made her appear all the more fabulous than she already was.

Lydia told Patrice about the letter opener (something that hadn't been mentioned in the news) and about Ellis Avery. By the time Lydia was finished, Patrice had finished cleaning her mixing bowls and was standing with her butt leaning against the center island, arms crossed over her chest, looking at Lydia.

"Tell me more about this detective," she said, peering intently at Lydia.

"There's not much to tell," Lydia said hastily. "He's from Yakima. Recently divorced, according to Misty."

"Hmmm," Patrice said. "There's something else about him. You like him, don't you?"

"He lives in Yakima," Lydia said stubbornly. "I'm not interested in a long-distance relationship."

"You won't actually know that until you try it," Patrice said, shrugging.

Patrice's husband Dan drove a huge semi for a national shipping company. He primarily worked up and down the west coast, rarely making cross-country trips. He was frequently gone for two to five days at a time. Patrice said it worked out great for them, and that he was going to have to build himself a second house if he ever retired, as Patrice was too used to living on her own for days at a time.

"He'll be here and gone," Lydia insisted. "Leave it, okay?"

"All right," Patrice said lightly, giving her a quick smile.

That was one of the reasons why Patrice was such a good friend to Lydia—she wasn't always insisting that Lydia needed to find someone. It was strange that she'd said anything about Ellis Avery.

Unless her friend really had seen something in Lydia that Lydia was busy denying.

"So why don't you instead tell me about you and Theo?" Lydia asked.

Patrice grinned at Lydia. "I was wondering when you'd get around to asking about that. A long, long time ago, back in high school, I may have had some sort of thing for your little brother."

"Really?" Lydia said. "I never knew!" The surprise made her sit up straighter in her chair, clutching the iced drink tighter in her hand.

"You weren't supposed to know," Patrice said, turning serious. "I never wanted you to doubt our friendship, that I was coming over to your house just to see Theo and not you. I kept the relationships strictly separate."

"You were in a relationship with Theo?" Lydia said. She couldn't have been more shocked. Not unless Patrice suddenly stripped off all her makeup and suddenly appeared homely and common.

"No, not really," Patrice said. "I was interested. He was, but he wasn't." She sighed. "There was more that happened, but I promised him I would never tell anyone. And I never have."

Lydia stared at her friend, stymied. She'd always known that Patrice would keep her word. It was one of the things her friend valued above anything else—being considered trustworthy.

"I won't ask you about anything more, then," Lydia said slowly.

Patrice gave her a huge smile. "Thank you. What I can tell you is that Theo had reasons for hating Schooner Thomas, more than the rest of us, because of what happened in high school."

Lydia sat frozen for a few moments, cup of coffee in her hand halfway to her lips. She thought back furiously to when she'd been a teenager. Did she remember anything happening with Theo and Principal Thomas? She shook her head and sipped her coffee, the chilled drink adding more goosebumps across her shoulders, despite the warmth of the ovens in the kitchen. No, she didn't remember anything. She'd been too caught up in her own teenaged drama.

"I can't tell you anything else," Patrice said. "You should ask him. He might finally be ready to tell you, now."

"It wasn't anything horrible, was it?" Lydia asked, her brain immediately leaping to the worst-case scenario, as always. "Like, abuse?" She didn't want to think about her little brother being abused while his big sister did absolutely nothing.

"No, no, no," Patrice assured her. "Nothing like that. Principal Thomas may have been a bigoted, misogynistic jerk, but he wasn't a child abuser."

"Good," Lydia said, taking a deep breath. She knew that small towns always had a lot of secrets, especially someplace that appeared as peaceful as Lake Hope did on the surface.

"So, who do you think killed Schooner Thomas?" Lydia asked, turning back to the speculation that everyone was chatting about.

"It could have been anyone, really," Patrice said. "But I don't think Theo did it."

Lydia blinked, surprised. She hadn't even considered that her brother might be guilty of such a thing. Then again, he'd changed over the last few years. She remembered how hollow he'd seemed when she'd first seen him. As if nothing was left inside.

"I'd never even considered him!" Lydia said. Really, Theo? No, that didn't make any sense.

"I know the timing's right," Patrice said seriously. "He'd just come into town. And your parents aren't here to account for his whereabouts."

"You don't think he's a suspect, do you?" Lydia asked. She couldn't vouch for him either. How could she protect him? Be the big sister she'd never been?

Patrice shrugged. "The police probably consider everyone a suspect. At least for now. You said they don't have an exact time of death yet?"

"I don't know," Lydia said. "I bet if I asked Misty, I could find out."

"She's got cousins in the Yakima coroner's office, doesn't she?" Patrice said with a grin.

"Cousin, in-law, something," Lydia said. It was one of the advantages of working with Misty—Lydia always knew what was going on with everyone in town. Frequently, any three counties if she had a few hours to check.

The two friends chatted a bit longer before Lydia had to get back to the B&B, to be there for her first guests. She gave Patrice a hug before she left. All this talk of Schooner's death and her brother had unsettled her. It was so nice to have a solid friend who didn't hold back, but who hugged her and held her until Lydia felt more grounded.

That was the one thing that Lydia missed: having a partner who held her.

While walking back to the B&B, Lydia texted her brother and invited him to the wine tasting she was planning

Friday night. It would make her parents happy that she'd thought to invite him.

Even if she had ulterior motives and was intending to give him the third degree about what had happened between him and Schooner Thomas.

12

"I had to go to the police station!" Alice announced when she came into the laundry room of the B&B Thursday afternoon.

"Really?" Lydia asked, surprised. Surely no one suspected Alice of killing Schooner Thomas? That would require a lot more planning than Alice was capable of. Wouldn't it? She handed Alice a warm sheet from the dryer as she pulled out another towel for herself to fold. The other dryer was still running its load, a familiar hum in the otherwise quiet room. The smell of fresh, warm cotton reminded Lydia of her mom and her claim that laundry was her artform, making her smile.

"The police asked me about Schooner," Alice said, automatically starting to fold up the sheet. "Why I didn't like him."

"Did you tell them the truth? About what he said about you?" Lydia said.

"I did!" Alice said. "He was mean to me. All the time."

"I wish you would have told me," Lydia said. "I would have told him that he couldn't come here anymore."

"I told Mama," Alice said. "She said not to tell you. She didn't want you losing any customers."

Lydia pressed her lips together so she wouldn't reply. She was going to have a talk with Jen McGowen later, when Alice wasn't there. Lydia could well have afforded to lose a customer like Schooner Thomas.

She also really wanted to know if there was someone else not being nice to Alice. She would be happy to lose another customer rather than Alice.

"The nice detective asked about the eggs," Alice admitted. "Someone saw me go to old Schooner's house. It was Friday night. I couldn't remember if it had been Friday or Saturday."

A cold shiver of fear ran down Lydia's back, despite the warmth of the pillowcase in her hands. "So a neighbor saw you go to Schooner Thomas's house?"

"They did," Alice nodded solemnly as she started folding another sheet. "They saw me go there and not leave."

"But you didn't go into the house, right?" Lydia said. The police surely would have dusted for fingerprints or something. That was something cops did. Right?

"That's right! I told them that." Alice finished her sheet and put it on the counter next to Lydia's stack of towels. "I was telling the truth," she said in a very quiet voice. "I'm not sure they believed me."

"I'm sure it will be fine," Lydia said automatically. No one would think Alice capable. Right?

"The detective did ask me to show them how strong I am," Alice said with a sudden grin. "I liked showing them that. I'm very strong!"

"Yes, yes you are," Lydia said, now more worried. According to Misty, the coroner believed that there had been an altercation in the house. Schooner had fallen or been pushed over, then smothered with a pillow.

Whoever held Schooner down would have to have been very strong. Plus, after he'd been smothered, someone had stabbed the letter opener into his chest. Again, it would have taken a lot of strength to do that as the opener was so blunt.

"Mama said it was good to tell them the truth," Alice said. "That the truth was the right thing. And Mitch said that I'm a Person of Interest!"

"Did Mitch hear that on his scanner?" Lydia said. That seemed unlikely. The police wouldn't just announce that where everyone could hear it, would they?

"No. He knows all about police stuff. It's for his book," Alice told her. "He explained the booking procedure and everything!"

"Wait. They didn't arrest you, did they?" Lydia said, suddenly confused.

"They told Mama we couldn't go on vacation," Alice said. "But we could go on picnics."

"I'm glad you can still go on picnics with your family," Lydia said. She cringed at the excited look on Alice's face, instantly regretting her words.

"You could come with us! Next Wednesday," Alice said. "So we don't work all the time."

"Maybe," Lydia said. She did want to talk with Jen McGowen, and possibly to Mitch as well, about whether or not other customers of hers were being mean to Alice.

The pair of them finished folding the clean laundry, then walked up the stairs to change over some of the rooms. Lydia kept thinking about the case, though.

No one would believe that Alice was capable of killing someone like Schooner Thomas. Right?

She was going to have to figure out how to talk with Detective Avery in private about that. It was just for Alice's sake. Not that she wanted to be closer to the man. Really.

13

Lydia was surprised to see the detective's name on the list of people attending the wine tasting Friday evening. Then again, maybe he wanted to experience some of the wines in the area without having to worry about drinking and driving. It was one of the reasons why Lydia offered the wine tastings at the B&B now and again. Most of the people who attended were staying with her, or were in walking distance, so she didn't have to worry too much about accidents.

She was happy that Theo had agreed to attend, though she suspected what had made him accept, at least in part, was that she'd waive the tasting fee for him. She wasn't about to pay for any bottles he might purchase, but she'd certainly let him try anything open for free.

That night, Lydia had gotten her friend Bill from the Blue Pond Winery to come and run the tasting. Bill was an older, jovial man, who could play Santa Claus all year round with his pink cheeks, button nose, and white beard and mustache. Bill's partner Peter was exactly the opposite, being tall, thin, dark, and somewhat dour.

As Blue Pond's tasting room was more than three hours away from Lake Hope, neither of the two regular bus tours of the local vineyards would include it. So Bill was usually amenable to coming into Lake Hope to do a tasting at Lydia's B&B. Lydia really liked their wines as well. During the week she didn't serve alcohol with breakfast or lunch, but on the weekends she'd serve mimosas in the mornings and beer in the afternoons.

One of the reasons why Lydia didn't bother serving wine at the restaurant was she could never choose which ones to serve. She didn't want to slight any of the local vineyards by only serving one variety, and she always felt overwhelmed by the sheer number of wines that were available. Plus, they changed all the time! No, better to just arrange tastings now and again, letting every vineyard who wanted to come in and serve.

Lydia had met Bill when she'd first come back to Lake Hope, almost ten years ago, though she'd known his partner Peter for ages. She'd considered working at a winery, maybe managing a wine tasting room. However, she was aware that she didn't make a good employee. She'd always been better working for herself. Something else that her ex, Neil, had never quite grasped.

Bill arrived just after six PM in a brand new van the winery had recently bought, with a wrap that covered the sides and back, advertising the winery and its wines. It was beautifully done, tastefully executed. Lydia knew Ed and Alan would have approved.

"Hi, Bill!" Lydia said, coming out of the kitchen and greeting him as he came into the restaurant. He wore one of his typical Hawaiian shirts, this one with a background of navy blue and decorated with bright yellow-orange pineapples. He was always threatening to retire someday to Hawaii, except that he was having too much fun here. His khaki shorts ended just above the knees, showing powerfully muscled legs.

Bill came over and gave her a great bear hug. It was comforting, like getting a hug from Ed or Alan. Bill was quite tall, and was easily able to put a kiss on the top of Lydia's head.

"How are you doing?" Bill asked, pulling back so he could look Lydia square in the eye.

"I'm fine," Lydia assured him, unsure why he seemed so concerned.

"We heard about the murder," Bill explained, shaking his head and letting go of Lydia after giving her biceps one last squeeze. "Horrible."

"It is," Lydia said. "I just keep hoping that it wasn't someone in town who did it." That was the one thought that continued to haunt her.

Bill tilted his head to the side. "But it's probably someone from near here, isn't it?" he said. "No one liked Schooner Thomas."

Lydia nodded. "I know. It's just my foolish hope." She paused, then asked, "How are you? How is Peter?"

Bill brightened up considerably. "We're fine. I've just opened up one of the new chardonnays for tasting before we bottle it. I think you'll like it."

"Excellent," Lydia said. "I've made room for the crates in the walk-in. And we'll have the same setup as usual—serve from behind the counter out here in the restaurant, with some cheese, crackers, fresh grapes, and salami."

"Good," Bill said. "I'll start bringing the crates in." He turned, paused, then turned back with a pensive look on his face. "There was something else I was supposed to tell you. Something about a guest."

Lydia looked blankly at him. "I don't know," she said after a few moments.

"Ack, it'll come back to me," Bill said, turning and leaving the restaurant.

Lydia smiled and shook her head. How typical of the older man, to almost remember something. He did it all the time.

She walked back into the kitchen and went back to slicing the cheese she'd be serving, arranging it artfully on pretty platters. Though she'd be helping Bill throughout the evening, restocking bottles as well as food plates, she hoped she'd be able to slip away long enough to talk both with Theo as well as Detective Avery.

That was the plan, at any rate.

The wine tasting started at seven. Theo was there promptly. He actually looked better, less haunted. He was still in dorky looking shorts and sandals, though at least his black T-shirt looked as though it fit him and wasn't a hand-me-down from a larger relative.

Was he so relaxed because he'd finally killed his archenemy?

Lydia chided herself for automatically leaping to the worst possible conclusion. No, her brother was probably relaxed because he'd been staying out on their parents' property. They had three-fourths of an acre, well maintained, with pyramid pines all around it, acting both as a wind break as well as a very effective privacy fence. The house itself wasn't much, three tiny bedrooms crammed into a thousand square feet. The outdoor porch was enclosed so they could use it year-round, giving them all much needed space.

"Hey, Lydia," Theo said. He actually came over to where she stood behind the counter, though he didn't hug her.

While Lydia hugged her parents regularly, she and Theo had never been that close.

He looked around the space. "Is there something I can help with?"

Lydia blinked, surprised. She'd always considered Theo the epitome of laziness. He *never* offered to help. Maybe Jasmine had finally whipped him into shape. Or an alien had stolen the original copy of Theo and this was a pod person she was talking to.

"Naw, we're good," she said. She introduced Theo to Bill, then turned to greet the next guests who'd come up to the counter.

Bill separated those coming in for the tasting into groups, easily keeping track of where everyone was in terms of the tasting menu. He'd printed several copies of the list of the wines being served tonight and walked people through the sequence, from light whites to heavier reds.

Lydia was always fascinated listening to him talk about the notes each wine had. While her palette was getting better, she knew that she'd never be able to match his. When he talked of blueberry and blackberry notes, all she got was berry.

The twelve people who were staying at the B&B attended the tasting that night, along with a few locals, plus another two dozen or so who came in off the street, either walking by or who had been told about the tasting. There were a couple of vacation rental owners who Lydia had sent an email to about the event, as well as the owner of the other B&B just up the street.

Lydia collected glasses and washed them regularly, resupplied Bill when bottles were nearly empty, and filled orders from the cases back in the kitchen.

It wasn't until near the end of the night that Lydia managed to have a private word with Theo. He'd spent the evening chatting with people, almost like an additional host. She'd seen him laughing more than once. It had startled her when she'd realized that she didn't remember the last time she'd heard him laugh.

But she found him alone, sipping a glass of the very fine Cabernet that Bill had brought. He sat at the table closest to the unlit fireplace, looking out on the room with a slight smile.

Lydia slipped into the chair beside him. "Some night, eh?"

Theo turned and grinned at her. "So this is what you do for excitement?"

Lydia nodded. "I work. Then I work some more."

Theo snorted. "I see that." Then he turned more serious. "You've got a good place here. Good people."

"Thanks," Lydia said, surprised but pleased that he'd noticed. She paused, then the words just came tumbling out. "You want to tell me what really brought you back to Lake Hope?"

Theo stiffened immediately.

Damn it! She should have waited. But Lydia had never been one to beat around the bush.

Theo appeared to make a decision and relaxed slightly. "I really did need to sort some things out. I'm still not ready to talk about it. But mainly, I needed to come back here and figure out what was real from my past and what was all in my head."

"Okay," Lydia said slowly. She'd experienced a little of that when she'd come back home after her divorce, things not being as she'd remembered. She had the impression, though, that Theo had something specific in mind, not just the streets being narrower or the lake being so much more peaceful than she'd remembered.

"Do you want to tell me what was going on with you and Patrice?" Lydia finally asked, figuring she should get all her questions out on the table. "I mean, it was obvious when you saw her that something was going on."

Theo looked pensive. "That, too, is something you're just

going to have to wait on. Along with what I had against Schooner Thomas." He paused, then raised his glass in a toast. "Here's to those finally dying who deserved it."

Lydia blinked, surprised at the vehemence in his voice. "You really hated him, didn't you?"

Theo nodded but didn't say anything more, just took another swig of wine from his glass. "And yes, the police have already contacted me about coming in for an interview. Appears my timing was perfect, coming into town when I did. With no one to vouch for my whereabouts Friday evening." He shrugged again. "I took a walk late that night. Someone spotted me in the neighborhood."

"Did you kill him?" Lydia said simply. She watched her brother carefully, looking to see if there was a flinch or some other sort of tell.

Theo looked directly at her. "I did not," he said distinctly. "Though I'd like to shake the hand of whoever did."

Lydia may not have been close to her brother, but she believed him. "Then we just have to make sure that the police understand that you didn't do it."

Theo blinked, a surprised look crossing his face. "Thanks, sis."

Lydia threw a skeptical look at him.

"No, I mean it. I'm not being sarcastic for once," Theo assured her. "It's…nice to know that you believe me. That you'd stick up for me. Not many people would."

"Then you have the wrong friends," Lydia declared.

"I'm just starting to appreciate that," Theo said. He pointed with his chin over her shoulder. "But I think you need to go play hostess with your other guests now."

Lydia turned around to see who Theo meant. Detective Avery sat all by himself in the opposite corner, closest to the door, looking pensively out the window.

"First, I need to clear the glasses in here," Lydia said.

"Then I'll go talk with him." She stood, then reached over and gave Theo her hand. "Friends for now?"

He nodded solemnly. "Friends for now. Maybe even siblings, later," he said as he shook her hand.

That brought a warm smile to Lydia's face. "Something to look forward to," she said as she turned away.

She doubted that she'd ever become good friends with her brother. Still, having more family around wouldn't be a bad thing.

14

*A*fter Lydia swept the room, clearing off all the used wine glasses and empty platters of cheese and meats, she came back out of the kitchen to find that most of the guests had left. There was one couple still at the counter, discussing with Bill about what to serve with one of the red blends they'd bought, another couple who were staying at the B&B who sat in the corner near the fireplace and talked quietly, and Detective Avery, who still sat close to the door, staring out at the street.

Lydia found her heart pounding as she thought about taking off her apron to go and talk with the man. Pensive was a good look on him. She could see how it could slide off into dark and brooding, but he hadn't crossed that line. At least, not yet.

Then she chided herself for acting out of character. He was a guest staying at her B&B. She'd never fraternized with any of her guests. And she wasn't about to. She kept her apron on and made herself walk casually over to his table.

"Good evening, Detective," Lydia said as casually as she could.

"Please, just Ellis tonight," he said, giving her a soft smile.

His eyes looked so deep. Lydia found herself drawn into them, sitting down at the table beside him without meaning to.

"Did you enjoy the tasting tonight? Were there any wines that were your favorites?"

Ellis gave her a smile that made wrinkles crinkle around his eyes, another good look on him.

"I did," he told her solemnly. "Bill gave me a taste of the new chardonnay, the one that isn't bottled yet. I was so tempted to put my name down on the list for a case once it's finished. But it would take me a year or more to go through so much wine. It doesn't seem worth it."

Lydia nodded. "I'm the same way. If I want some wine, I can always go just down the street and get an extraordinarily good glass of it. I don't need to keep any here."

"That being said, Bill was very persuasive about the very fine red blend he's serving, offering a discount on a half case," Ellis said.

"That is tempting," Lydia said sincerely. "Bill must have liked you. Blue Pond doesn't usually do half cases."

"I'm going to think about it," Ellis said. "It's still a lot of wine to drink all by myself."

Lydia made herself sit back a little in her chair so that she wouldn't automatically offer to drive up to Yakima and drink some of the wine with him.

"How is the case going?" she asked. Then she held her hands up. "I know you can't really tell me any details."

"Then you know I can't really tell you how it's going," Ellis said. "Though I suspect that most people in town already have a pretty good idea of the exact status of where we stand. Particularly part of your staff here, Misty Martìnez?"

Lydia couldn't help but snort. "It's a small town," she said, spreading her hands wide. "And Misty has a large extended family."

"I've met the type before," Ellis said dryly. "So we're actually being more open with this case than we usually would be."

"That's just to get people to stop bugging you for information, isn't it?" Lydia said. At Ellis's look, she asked, "What?"

"Small towns," he said, shaking his head. "I grew up in George, north and east of here."

"They have the huge cherry pie every year, don't they?" Lydia asked. "At the fourth of July?"

Ellis looked surprised. "Not many people know about that."

Lydia shrugged. "I run a B&B. I'm always looking for activities to tell tourists about. Local things that they can go to."

"That makes sense," Ellis said, nodding. "So what do you want to know about the case?"

"Am I that transparent?" Lydia said, teasing.

"It's a small town," Ellis said.

"You don't really believe that Alice McGowen is capable of killing anyone, do you?" Lydia had to ask. "She isn't capable of such a thing."

"Why do you say that?" Ellis asked, much more formal than he had been.

Lydia watched a veneer of "police detective" come down over Ellis's formerly deep (and, okay, dreamy) eyes. He was still Ellis Avery—the change was subtle. It was as if he'd just shifted slightly to the left, his entire persona no longer open and carefree.

Part of her wanted to apologize for taking him back into that mode. But the rest of her needed to speak her piece.

"Alice isn't organized enough to have planned something like that in advance," Lydia said. "She's much more spontaneous, not that meticulous."

Ellis nodded. "Yet, she was able to save up rotten eggs for a week, just so she could go and throw them at Schooner Thomas's house."

"I bet if you ask carefully, you'll find that she didn't actually have a reason for saving up the eggs, not until she thought to throw them that night," Lydia countered.

Ellis gave nothing away. "And what if the killing was spontaneous? A crime of passion, and not planned?"

"It still wasn't Alice," Lydia insisted. "Yes, she's strong enough to have done it, from what I understand. But she knows what's right and what's wrong, and she knows killing is just wrong."

"But she helps her parents out at their farm all the time," Ellis said. "Kills chickens. Looks forward to fresh lard from the hogs they'll butcher this fall."

Lydia sighed. "I know all that. But she just wouldn't have done it."

Ellis gave her a bemused smile. "That's what people say about killers all the time." Then he grew more serious. "Who would have done it? If you're so certain Alice didn't?"

"I don't know," Lydia said honestly. "I just can't believe it would be anybody in town. Nobody liked Schooner much. But no one hated him enough to kill him."

"Yet, someone did," Ellis pointed out.

Before Lydia could respond, she heard Bill softly call her name.

She stood up, but paused for a moment. "It wasn't Alice. And it wasn't Theo, my brother. I swear it wasn't."

Ellis merely shrugged. "I'm going to have to go where the evidence leads me."

Lydia could read between the lines easily enough to hear

the unspoken words—that right at the moment, it didn't look good for Alice.

"Have a nice evening," Lydia told Ellis before she walked back to where Bill stood. He asked her to package up another couple of bottles for him while he took care of the last of the tastings.

Lydia walked pensively back into the kitchen. Alice hadn't killed Schooner Thomas, no matter what Ellis might think. Neither had Theo, though she knew the police suspected him as well.

Whoever had done it needed to step forward and admit it, so that life in Lake Hope could return to some semblance of normal. That was all there was to it.

15

*L*ydia helped Bill reload the van with the last of the cases that hadn't sold. As usual, the evening had cooled off considerably, to the point where Lydia grabbed a sweater before she stepped out. Stars peeked out of the dark sky, visible even with the few streetlights that shone. Music interrupted the quiet, coming from *The Point* —a bar down the street—something much too loud and fast for her tastes. The air still carried a taste of hot asphalt from earlier that day, another promise of the summer heat still to come.

It had been a good night. At least half the cases Bill had brought with him were now empty.

"I saw you sitting with that detective earlier," Bill said as he closed the van's doors.

"Just curious about the case, like everyone else," Lydia said lightly.

"Don't try to lie to this old poker player," Bill said with mock seriousness. "The sparks you two were throwing could have lit the place on fire."

Lydia rolled her eyes at him. "He's a detective first," she

said after a few moments. "I doubt any of us will ever see the real him."

"I'm not too sure about that," Bill said. "Oh! That reminds me! What I'd wanted to tell you earlier!"

"Yes?" Lydia said when Bill didn't instantly continue.

"Peter thought he saw Neil, your ex, out at the wine room last week," Bill said. "He wasn't positive. But he thought it was Neil. Was asking if we sold any beer," Bill added with an eye roll.

Lydia felt as though her entire world had suddenly slipped, as if she'd just drunk a full bottle of wine all on her own. The stars seemed to whirl above her, and the music from down the street suddenly clashed, loud and discordant.

"Really?" she asked. "Why the hell would he come back here? He hated it here, hated Lake Hope. Was so glad to shake the dust off his shoes when we landed in Seattle."

That had been a huge part of their problem. Lydia had always remained close to her parents. Neil hadn't. They'd ended up with huge screaming matches before the start of any holiday, when Lydia wanted to leave Seattle and come back to Lake Hope to visit her family.

"Don't know," Bill said. "Figured he'd be coming to see you."

"Why would he do that?" Lydia said, honestly confused. "He loves Seattle. Hell, one of the last things that Neil did was to threaten to get 'even' with me for ruining his life." Neil had always been something of a drama queen. He also frequently blamed other people for his problems instead of addressing them himself.

In fact, now that she was thinking about it, she realized that he'd hated Schooner Thomas as well, and had made the same threats about getting even with him. The principal had refused to write letters of recommendation for Neil back in the day. He'd blamed not getting into the first college of his choice on that, instead of on the fact that he'd nearly flunked out of calculus. Twice.

Bill shrugged. "Is there something going on with his family, then?"

"I'll ask Misty, tomorrow," Lydia said. She hadn't kept in touch with Neil's family. They hadn't wanted anything to do with her when she'd come back to Lake Hope, not after their precious son had thrown her to the curb. At least they'd mostly kept their opinions to themselves and hadn't actively tried to ruin her B&B.

Bill nodded. He took a deep breath then let it go. "Come out and see us sometime," he said seriously. "While it's quiet here, it's even more peaceful out at the vineyard."

Bill and Peter had put her up for a weekend once, while she'd been trying to decide about running their tasting room for them. It had been a little too quiet out there for Lydia.

"Thanks," Lydia said. "I'll keep that in mind. Maybe in September, when I close the B&B and go on vacation…"

"Sounds like a plan," Bill said, giving her one last long hug.

Lydia soaked up all the comfort she could before returning back to the B&B and closing up for the night.

Yes, she loved her place, and the work she did. But maybe it would be good to get away for a while, later.

Humming, she grabbed herself a large glass from the bottle of the new chardonnay that Bill had left her, then made her way back to her rooms, content to sit and sip wine and maybe read something for the rest of the evening. She needed a distraction, to forget about potential siblings and detectives with dreamy eyes.

As well as an ex who'd come back to haunt her.

---

16

*L*ydia woke up angry. Her jaw hurt because she'd been clenching her teeth all night. Even her muscles were sore from being so tense. She stretched while still lying on her bed, sticking her arms out of the warm cocoon of covers, then drawing them back in again. During the summer, she slept with a window partially open, keeping the room cool so she could pile on the blankets.

It took her a couple of moments to figure out what was wrong, why rage boiled in her chest like an angry thunderbolt looking for a target. It wasn't the murder, though that didn't help. It wasn't that she was tired of working all the time, though that stress did add to her troubles. It wasn't even that she knew that she and Ellis would never have a chance at a relationship.

No. It was the possibility that Neil had returned to Lake Hope.

This was *her* hometown. Yes, he might have come from here originally, just as she had. But he'd disowned it. Had never wanted to come back here, even for vacations. Rarely talked with his family. She could just hear his snide remarks about her chosen career—how she might call herself a hotelier but that just meant she cleaned toilets for a living.

Damn it! He was not allowed to come here and ruin her life.

She snorted at herself as she sat up in bed. Right. Because his coming here was going to make a mess of everything.

Lydia looked around her bedroom. When she'd built the addition, and then decorated it, she'd made every design decision based on whether the result would delight her or not. It wasn't good enough to just be pretty or functional. No, it had to be both, as well as delightful.

So the ceiling was slanted, the high point being over the door in the far corner, the wall above her headboard the shortest. Beautiful cedar wood made up the ceiling, coated with a shiny varnish but unstained, so the natural beauty shone through and it reflected light, which made the room seem even brighter. She'd painted the walls a soothing gray-blue that changed colors as the light shifted during the day, making the room seem different all the time. The floors were a manufactured hardwood, stained a rich mahogany, an elegant contrast to everything else. She'd reclaimed the dresser she'd grown up with from her parents, stripped off the white paint to reveal the beautiful cherry wood underneath.

Her walls held a few pictures of family, a beautiful painting of New York that Ed and Alan had given her, and a cork board where she put special postcards that she received from her guests, pictures from their hometowns or other places they visited. Everything was chic but still homey.

Lydia made herself take a deep breath, trying to let go of her anger. Despite her shoulders dropping, her toes and fists still curled.

Nope. Relaxation wasn't going to happen. She was going to be pissed off about Neil coming to *her* hometown for a while yet.

She sighed and pushed herself off her bed, leaning down to touch her toes, stretching out her back. She should really start going to yoga class every evening again, though honestly, most nights she felt too tired by the time classes started.

Maybe after the busy season was over. For now, she needed to get ready for her day.

And prepare herself for when she crossed paths with her ex again.

*L*ydia tried to take satisfaction in chopping grapes, strawberries, and melons, but it wasn't enough. No, she still wanted to take her sharpest knife and just skewer Neil. Followed closely by skinning whoever it was who'd killed Schooner Thomas. Then maybe a little light torture of Ellis Avery as well, for disrupting her nice, calm, placid life.

Had Neil come back and killed Schooner? That didn't seem to be in character for her ex. While on the one hand, he'd talked frequently about getting revenge on this person or that. On the other hand, he'd never gotten off his ass and done anything.

Then again, he had been the one to ask for the divorce. Lydia had known that there were problems with their marriage. She hadn't been happy. She'd still been completely surprised when he'd served papers on her.

Lydia tried to give Misty a big smile when she came into the kitchen. While Lydia had dressed in tans and pinks that day in an effort to cheer herself up, Misty wore dark colors, looking somber.

Misty took one look at Lydia and asked, "Wake up on the wrong side of the bed this morning?"

Lydia sighed and put the knife down so she wouldn't chop off a finger or something. "That obvious?"

"When you bare your teeth at me like that, yeah," Misty said with a laugh. "Anything I can do to help?"

"Well," Lydia said slowly. She was sometimes hesitant to tap into Misty's wide network of contacts, in part because she didn't want to know just how far of a reach the other woman had. "Bill told me that Peter had seen Neil out at the wine tasting room last week."

Misty blinked, looking surprised. "Really?"

Lydia could see the woman running through her Rolodex of gossip and information.

"Okay, as far as I know his parents are fine," Misty said after a few moments. "But I can check with the receptionist at their doctor's office and make sure."

"Is that legal?" Lydia asked. "Isn't that a HIPAA violation or something?"

Misty just waved a hand, as if clearing away any doubts. "Close enough," she said. "It's a small town. Someone saw them going to the clinic if they went. But I won't be able to do any real checking until Monday."

Lydia nodded. "Okay. Thank you," she said. She sighed. "I'd really like to know what that asshole is doing here." Because of course her mind leaped to the worst possible conclusion, that he'd come here to ruin her life.

"You got it, boss," Misty said. She came around to the other side of the counter, picking up the knife. "Now, before you hurt yourself or someone else, why don't you go make coffee and set the tables up? I'll take care of the rest of the prep."

"Thank you," Lydia said, more relieved than she'd expected. She and Misty swapped responsibilities on a regular basis, so it wasn't as if she'd never done service out front before. But today, she just couldn't be in the kitchen.

In fact, she felt the need to get out of the B&B altogether.

Lydia kept a polite smile in place as she greeted the people drifting into the restaurant. Ellis Avery was up early, having his usual eggs, bacon, fruit salad, and tea. Lydia treated him the same as everyone else, ignoring the way she wanted to run her fingertips along his smooth chin, as well as how she wanted to drift just a little closer to get a better smell of his aftershave. He held himself just as aloof, that veneer of police detective firmly in place, the man hidden behind that smoky wall.

It was just Lydia's imagination that she felt his eyes following her as she made her way across the busy restaurant, serving her customers and bussing tables so the next guests could come and sit down.

All the tables filled up and she even had a waiting list for a while, due to tourists coming in from other hotels. It was mornings like this when she wished she could hire someone else to help in the restaurant. However, she wasn't usually this busy. Having more help was an expense she couldn't afford, as much as she needed the extra hands that day.

The breakfast rush cleared out around eleven. It appeared that no one wanted lunch. Which was good, as both Lydia and Misty needed a bit of breathing room. There were only two rooms changing over that night—everyone else was staying for the weekend and wouldn't leave until Sunday.

After Lydia had brought down the linens from the rooms and started the laundry, she turned around, looking at the four walls of the laundry room. The two stacks of industrial machines took up the back wall, their quiet humming a constant source of pride. In front of Lydia was the folding table, built to her specifications, so it was exactly the right height for doing laundry on. She kept the B&B seasonal decorations stored back here, neatly ordered in labeled plastic bins. She was going to have to dig out the Fourth of July bin next weekend, put up all the flags and pennants.

Lydia didn't feel trapped in the room, not exactly. But those walls were kind of closing in on her.

She walked back to the kitchen. There just wasn't much to do at that point. No new customers had come in to eat lunch. Misty could handle the two couples who were there. All the dishes had been done and put away from the morning rush. Misty was chatting on the phone in Spanish with one of her numerous relatives.

Maybe Lydia could go do some weeding, out behind the building? No, that didn't sound appealing at all. She'd never understood her mother's need to garden.

Misty finished off her conversation just then. "There's a package at the post office that you should go pick up," she said. She crossed her arms over her chest and stared intently at Lydia. "Now."

Lydia got the message. "Yes, Mom," she said with an exaggerated sigh, though she knew that getting out of the B&B, actually leaving the premises for a while, was the best thing she could do.

"You could also pick up the pastries for tomorrow from *The Palace*," Misty said. "After you come back."

"Thank you," Lydia said, smiling. She was happy to be out running errands today.

"I'll hold down the fort," Misty said. "And I'll text you if we get a lunch rush or something. For now—just go."

Lydia nodded. She knew that her restlessness was mostly due to the left-over anger at Neil. She couldn't wait to get the inevitable confrontation with him over with. She turned and marched right out of the B&B and into the street. It was sunny, bright, and quiet. Right now that felt good, though Lydia knew she'd miss the rain after a few more weeks of this.

Few cars were parked, and fewer tourists were ambling down the sidewalk. Good. That meant an even quieter day.

Since Misty had everything so well in hand, and the tourists appeared to be cooperating, maybe Lydia could go hunting Neil.

Thus equipped with her tasks, Lydia strode down the street with great determination. To pick up the mail, get the pastries, and find her ex.

And tell him to get the hell out of her hometown.

17

The post office was in yet another new building on the opposite side of town from the B&B. During Lydia's lifetime, it had move three times. When she'd been a girl, the post office had been in one of the older buildings in downtown proper, on Main Street. However, while the building was regal looking, made up of a yellowish brick, with marble floors and brass fixtures on the inside, it had never been well maintained. During a particularly wet spring, the entire roof had collapsed. Lydia remembered mourning the building, along with her parents, as it had been so pretty.

The post office had moved to a temporary location just a few blocks away, into a converted department store. When Lydia had gone there with her mother as a teen, she remembered that there were always cardboard boxes of supplies piled up against the walls, making the front office area tiny.

While Lydia had been away, a brand-new post office building had finally been erected, where an old parking lot had been. It didn't have the character of the first building, but the roof was solid. And chances were, the post office would be there for a good long time.

This post office always seemed dim to Lydia, with the only bright lights shining on the workers behind the counter. A long line snaked through the open area, people mailing packages or picking up their mail on a Saturday. Lydia joined the line, a little restless still, though the walk all the way through downtown to the other side had done her good.

Joseph Tiwali stood in line in front of her. He owned the single car repair shop in town, and wore a light-blue shirt with thin white stripes, with his name embroidered above the left pocket. He smelled of oil and gears, like her dad now often did since he'd retired and started working as a handyman. Joseph had an easy smile and a friendly nature, and had gone through three wives over the years. He had at least four children, possibly more if the gossip was to be believed.

There wasn't a gas station in Lake Hope—you had to go out to the highway for that. Joseph did a good business either towing cars or bringing gas to those who got stranded. He'd been a few years ahead of her in high school.

"Heard any news about the murder?" he asked, turning slightly to chat with her. He had a three-foot stack of packages at his feet, all carefully wrapped and already labeled.

"The police are still investigating all possibilities," Lydia said, carefully choosing her words. Joseph didn't deserve any of her anger at either Neil or at Ellis Avery.

"Can't get that detective to talk, huh?" he teased. It didn't surprise Lydia that Joseph knew that the detective was staying at her B&B. That was old news at this point.

"They aren't telling anyone anything," Lydia said with a smile. She actually was kind of glad that the police were taking the situation seriously, respecting Schooner Thomas's privacy. "So how are your girls?" she asked in return.

All four of Joseph's kids were girls between the ages of three and ten. He doted on them and was always happy to talk about their latest exploits. At least for now. Lydia suspected that matters might change dramatically once they reached dating age.

Joseph kept Lydia entertained with stories about hunting for frogs at the lake and being fascinated by the minnows at the shallow end, as the line crept forward. It wasn't until Joseph picked up his packages and carried them up to the counter that Lydia looked around at the other people in the post office.

Wait a second. The man just leaving. He looked familiar.

"Next!" Gina called, waving to get Lydia's attention.

Crap. Lydia didn't want to just bolt out the door of the post office to follow him. The line hadn't gotten any shorter —people coming in and replacing everyone who'd been served.

It couldn't have been Neil. Could it?

No. Not unless he'd changed dramatically over the last few years. Neil was proud, possibly overly so, and held his head high. That poor individual carried himself in a slouch with his head down and shoulders forward.

"Next," Gina said, her voice carrying a warning as she waited for Lydia.

"Right, sorry," Lydia said as she walked forward and handed the clerk the slip of paper about the package waiting for her.

When Gina came back, Lydia had to ask. "The guy before me, that wasn't Neil Roswell, was it?"

"Who?" Gina asked. Then she shook her head. "Don't know."

Lydia sighed, remembering that Gina had only started working at the post office the previous year and had no idea who Neil might be.

"Thanks," Lydia said as she picked up her package. It wasn't that big—maybe a foot wide and half that tall. However, it felt heavy enough that she knew she needed to carry it in two hands. She nodded again to Joseph and made her way out the door.

Once Lydia walked back to Main Street, she carefully looked around, seeing if she could spot that stranger. She didn't see him but she kept a careful eye out all the way back to the B&B, just in case.

18

The coasters were perfect, ceramic with cork bottoms, the words "Nip and Bud, Lake Hope" written in that beautiful purple that matched the local agates. Lydia doubted that she would sell many, which is why she had only ordered a dozen. Misty had plans to divide them up into sets of four, with beautiful purple ribbons tied around them. The weight in the box had come from the rest of her order, with four sturdy coffee mugs and a dozen keychain pendants.

Lydia eagerly stepped out of the B&B again after helping Misty with the rest of the lunch guests, walking to Patrice's bakery to pick up supplies for tomorrow morning's breakfast. While some guests would spend the time to have a full breakfast, she always found that Sunday mornings people were more likely to order pastries and coffee to go, eager to get on the road again.

Lydia looked around as she slowly walked up Main Street, looking for Neil. Or that stranger.

Had Peter seen the stranger and thought that it was Neil? She wasn't sure.

Oh! There he was! Window shopping at the consignment store just across the street! Same dark hair, black T-shirt, and gray shorts.

Lydia stepped out into the street without looking. The honk made her step back right away.

"Sorry! Sorry!" she said as the car roared past her. Really, she was just going to have to be more careful.

Where had he gone? Oh! There! Lydia checked for traffic both ways before she darted across the street and then walked rapidly up the sidewalk.

It was Neil! She was sure of it. Same arrogant nose and disapproving look.

"What are you doing here?" Lydia said, the words pouring out of her mouth before she could stop them. She'd meant to say hi. Or something.

"Excuse me?"

The young man who turned to look at her was not, in fact, Neil. Particularly not with that charming British accent. His eyes were gray, not brown, and his face was actually longer than Neil's.

"Oh, I'm so sorry! I thought you were my ex," Lydia said. She normally didn't blush, but she felt her cheeks grow warm.

The young man gave her a wan smile. "Right, then," he said, nodding at her then deliberately walking away, obviously not wanting to engage the crazy person.

Lydia sighed. She didn't know if she was disappointed that she hadn't found Neil or glad, knowing that she was likely to just yell at him when she did see him.

If she found him.

Slowly, Lydia walked up the street toward *The Palace*, looking this way and that, but she didn't see anyone else who looked like Neil. It was still quiet that morning, only a few couples holding hands, one older couple enjoying their retirement, even a young family with two kids, trying to tire the young ones out before they got back in the car.

Both Grace and Patrice were at the bakery, and there were a few customers ahead of Lydia. Patrice must have just finished baking more of her quick bread cakes, as the smell of lemon and cinnamon filled the air. Lydia didn't pace at the back of the store waiting for her turn, though she wanted to. Her stomach grumbled, hungry for lunch or anything sweet. She kept a smile plastered on her face even when one of the tourists stopped to chat about how pretty the lake had been that morning.

Damn it! Lydia still had other things to do.

"We've got your order," Patrice said as she finished with the previous customer. She walked into the kitchen in the back, then came out with a canvas bag already full.

"Thanks," Lydia said. Patrice kept meticulous records and sent Lydia an invoice every month, which Lydia paid promptly. It was one of the ways that they maintained their friendship, by generally charging for their services. That didn't mean that they wouldn't comp each other or give a "friends and family" rate. But Lydia tried not to ask for too many favors, and Patrice did the same. Neither wanted to feel as though she were being taken advantage of.

"Any news?" Patrice asked as she lifted the bag up over the counter.

"Neil's been spotted," Lydia admitted. She appreciated how wide her friend's eyes got.

"What's he doing here?" Patrice said.

It warmed Lydia's heart that Patrice sounded as outraged as Lydia had been. "No idea," she said. "Just keep an eye out and let me know if you see him."

"Will do," Patrice said grimly. She glanced around the bakery, then gave a shrug to Lydia. There were still at least a half dozen customers waiting. They couldn't talk just then.

Lydia smiled and nodded, showing that she understood. They could chat later.

Feeling bolstered, Lydia took the long way back to the B&B, walking around a few blocks before heading back to Main Street. She kept a careful eye out, looking for Neil but not wanting to make a mistake again. However, no one resembling him was walking in the bright sunlight.

Maybe on Monday, Misty could shed some light on what was going on, why he'd come back to town.

Lydia sighed as she walked back into the B&B. She was determined to spend the afternoon out in the back, destroying the few weeds that were growing there. Anything but spend the day inside, brooding.

Maybe she'd even make it to yoga class tonight as well. Or, failing that, perhaps have some more of Bill's very good wine to help her relax.

19

———

*L*ydia woke Sunday morning feeling groggy. She had a headache at the back of her skull, as if she a had crick in her neck. She shook her head and tried to wake up. She'd only had a single glass of wine the night before, so she wasn't hungover. But she just felt off. Lethargic.

After taking a long hot shower, Lydia finally felt better, but that nagging headache wouldn't go away. And there was the smell of something rotten in the air as well.

Lydia walked from her rooms down the hallway and into the restaurant. Normally, she would have gone straight into the kitchen. However, something caught her eye.

The door leading outside was ajar.

Had a guest been out late last night and somehow left it open? That was unlikely. Lydia had a strong mechanism on the door so that it would shut automatically. Sure, it was possible that someone could have left it open deliberately. But they would have had to work at it. She didn't see a stone or anything to keep the door open.

Lydia sighed and pushed the door shut. It gave an odd

click as she closed it. Ah. Maybe something was stuck in the door jam. She'd have to look at it later.

As Lydia made her way back to the kitchen, the awful odor grew stronger. It smelled like rotten eggs. Had the power gone out? Or had something gone wrong with the walk-in? No, it would have taken longer than over night for the eggs there to go bad.

Only when Lydia was in the kitchen did she hear the hissing noise.

The gas on the stove had been turned on and was running high.

Crap!

Lydia raced around the prep area to the stove, turning off all the burners and the grill as well. Then she opened up the two small windows in the kitchen that overlooked the garden in the back, as well as the ones out front in the restaurant.

Why hadn't the carbon monoxide alarms gone off? She had one in the kitchen as well as on every floor. She grabbed the step stool and was reaching for the first one when she realized that the light on it was no longer blinking.

Slowly, Lydia drew her hand back.

Danny had done her bi-annual inspection of all of the alarms in the B&B, as well as her fire extinguishers, in February. It was only June. The batteries wouldn't have worn out by now.

No, someone had deliberately turned on the gas. And it appeared that they had sabotaged the alarms as well.

Was someone trying to kill her? Had her ex finally gone ahead and actually done something in order to get his revenge on her?

Lydia shivered all the way to her core. She felt nauseated, and not just from the stink of the gas.

One stray spark, and the entire B&B would have gone up

in flames. It was an old building. Sure, she'd brought it up to code. That didn't mean it wouldn't have burned down.

Lydia looked around the kitchen, trying to see if anything else was out of place. Everything else seemed in order.

With heavy feet, Lydia turned and walked up the stairs. She paused on the second floor, checking the ceiling.

The carbon monoxide alarm was missing. Whoever had done this had just stolen it.

Same with the third floor.

Lydia shivered again, then headed straight for the Marigold room. She paused in the hallway, listening at the door. Yes, it sounded as though someone was already up. She knocked softly.

"Who is it?" called a deep voice from inside.

"Lydia," she said, identifying herself. She blamed the way her pulse raced on the fact that she'd just nearly been killed, not because she wanted to see the detective again.

"Yes?" Ellis said, opening the door and sticking his head out. He was awake, but obviously hadn't been for long, as his dark hair was tousled and his face still sleep creased. He wore a white T-shirt that was probably old, due to the way it stretched tightly across his chest, showing the muscles there. In addition, he had on a pair of gray sweatpants but his feet were bare, looking vulnerable against the soft brown of the rug.

"Can I come in for a moment?" Lydia asked, her voice not much louder than a whisper. She was well aware of how sound traveled between the rooms up here.

The detective held the door open further, letting her in. Lydia didn't speak until after he'd closed it.

"There was a break-in last night," she said, keeping her voice low.

Ellis grew very still, as if gathering himself up, winding

himself tighter so he could spring into action. "Was anything taken?"

"No," Lydia said. She sighed. She knew she was doing the right thing telling the detective, but she found she was still so shaken by it all. "Someone took the carbon monoxide alarms, at least up here. Then they turned on the gas on all the burners on the stove, just letting them run."

That seemed to surprise Ellis. The detective melted away and suddenly Lydia was facing the man again.

"Are you okay?" he asked, reaching out a warm hand to squeeze her bicep.

Lydia mutely nodded. This…attack, for want of a better word, had left her extremely unsettled.

Ellis did not sweep her into his arms to hug her. Lydia could see it in his eyes, how he'd thought about it, how his body had shifted closer, how he'd almost automatically done it.

Instead, he seemed to realize that he was touching her and dropped his hand, taking a deliberate step back. The veneer of the detective came slamming down again.

"The front door was left open," Lydia added. "I need to check the jam because it wasn't closing all the way anymore."

"I'll come with," Ellis volunteered. "Just give me a minute to get dressed."

Lydia nodded and let herself out of the detective's room. She took a deep breath, letting go of the wonderful masculine scent that she'd been unconsciously bathing in.

No, this wouldn't do. She was already off balance. She needed to pull herself together.

He would be leaving soon, heading back to Yakima.

Ellis slipped out of his room a moment later. He'd put on socks and sneakers, as well as a soft-looking flannel shirt over his T-shirt, though he'd kept his sweatpants on. He had a large black bag in his hand.

Lydia silently pointed at the empty bracket, where the missing carbon monoxide alarm normally resided. Ellis nodded, showing he understood. Then he opened his bag and took out a camera. He snapped a few pictures of the empty bracket, then nodded at her again. Lydia led him down the stairs. She was impressed at how quietly he moved, carefully placing his feet. She bet that would make him a good dancer. Not as though she ever had time to go dancing anymore.

After a quick stop on the second floor, taking more pictures, Lydia and Ellis first went to the front door. It turned out that a wadded up piece of paper had been slipped into the hole in the strike plate, where the door latch was supposed to go. It made it appear as though the door was closed. Without moving the handle or unlocking it, the door could just be pushed open. During the night, winds had probably pushed it open.

"Simple, effective," Ellis said as he knelt down to look at the wad of paper. "Easy to do without anyone noticing, particularly if you had the piece of paper ready. Could just slid it into the hole when passing either in or out of the door."

"Making it easy for someone without a key to gain access," Lydia said. She was proud of how steady her voice sounded.

Ellis studied the door jamb intently for a few moments, then turned to look up at Lydia.

"I should declare this as a crime scene," he said softly. "Call in a forensics team from Yakima."

"How long would that take?"

Ellis shrugged. "It's Sunday. I might be able to get someone out here by Monday. But more likely, Tuesday." He gestured to the empty restaurant. "You'd have to close the place. Probably the entire B&B."

"I can't do that," Lydia said immediately, panic clawing at her throat. "Where will my guests go?"

"Are there other inns they could stay at?" Ellis said.

"No. It's June. The whole town is full," Lydia said. She made herself take a deep breath so she didn't start yelling. "I was talking with one of the other innkeepers just down the street. Every room in all of Lake Hope is booked from now through August." Since Ellis had taken up her one free space, she, too, was booked up.

Ellis continued to stare mutely at her.

"Can't you just do everything yourself? Then you wouldn't have to call in a team," Lydia said. She would *not* close her B&B. The news would get out and she'd lose business. Not just in the short term, either. It might be enough to shut her down completely.

Was that the actual reason why someone had done this? To shut her down?

"It would be highly irregular for me to process the scene on my own," Ellis said. He gave her a grin. "It's part of why my superiors are pissed at me. Because that's exactly the sort of thing that I would do."

"Please?" Lydia said. "I can't close down. It will ruin me." She found herself quaking inside. This was worse, somehow, than the place burning down.

Ellis sighed, then nodded. "All right. I'll do it myself. You just need to understand that this may not hold up in court, as I'm not an expert."

Lydia thought for a moment. "Chances are, I won't care. It won't matter."

"Why is that?"

"Because whoever did this probably also killed Schooner Thomas. You'll need to convict them of murder, not just attempted murder."

"We don't know that for certain," Ellis warned.

"I know," Lydia said. "But chances are, that's what happened." She felt the connection deep in her gut.

"Can you think of anyone who would want to do you harm?" Ellis asked.

Lydia grimaced, then sighed. She chose her words carefully.

"My ex has supposedly just come back into town. I haven't seen him yet. And while it was, shall we say, an acrimonious divorce, this seems out of character for him. He'd rather humiliate me publicly, not sneak in and kill me. He wants to get even with me. Not murder me."

"Those feelings could have changed. Grown," Ellis said warned. "I've seen it happen."

Lydia nodded, unhappy. Neil had hated Schooner Thomas. Had something finally tipped him over the edge, turning him from a talker into a killer?

Ellis pursed his lips and thought for a moment. "All right. I'll document everything, but the paperwork about this aspect of the case may not get filed immediately."

"Thank you," Lydia said, relief cascading down her spine, replacing some of the chill that had taken root there.

"Don't thank me yet," Ellis said, drawing a notebook and pencil out of his bag. "We still haven't caught whoever's done this. Not yet."

His warm smile made Lydia's breath catch.

No, not yet. Nothing could happen yet.

But maybe, soon.

***

*L*ydia watched Ellis as he did a quick sketch of the paper in the door jamb. He explained that drawing the scene would force him to really see all the details.

She could see that. Though he was no great artist, it did look better than what she would have done.

And she was *not* about to tease him and ask for him to sign it and give it to her once the mystery was solved.

Then Ellis photographed the paper in the hole, both close up and from a distance, using a ruler to show the size. Afterward, he used a pair of tweezers to pry the paper out, slipping it into a plastic evidence bag, sealing the bag, signing and dating it.

"Will you get any fingerprints from that?" Lydia asked.

"I doubt it," Ellis said. "The surface isn't smooth. But I can send it to the techs in Yakima to see if they can pull anything from it." He sighed. "It doesn't make sense to try to fingerprint the door. There are too many people coming and going."

Ellis took a few more minutes to photograph the rest of the restaurant, drawing a quick sketch of it as well. Lydia couldn't see anything amiss. Except, of course, that it was getting late and she still had prep work to do. She tried to control her anxiety and let Ellis do his job.

In the kitchen, Ellis stopped and took more photographs. "Is this just how you found it?" he asked.

"No," Lydia said. "I turned off the gas. Opened the windows. Then I moved the stepstool so I could look at the alarm on the ceiling."

"Was the stepstool in the usual place?" Ellis said.

"I think so," Lydia said, thinking back. "I don't remember. I was in a panic."

"It's okay," Ellis said. He took out his sketch pad again and did a quick drawing of the kitchen, noting both where the stepstool had been moved to and where Lydia thought she had found it. Then he photographed the alarm. Before he took it down, he wrapped tape around the edges of it, then pulled it off and examined it.

"Clean," he said after a moment. "No fingerprints." Ellis paused, looking up at the alarm. "You couldn't take that alarm down without touching the edges of it. So whoever did it either wore gloves or wiped the prints off afterward. This is actually a good thing."

"Why is that?" Lydia said, not following the detective's logic.

"Even if I'd declared this a crime scene, and gotten a tech crew out here, they wouldn't have gotten much from it," Ellis said.

"Oh," Lydia breathed out a sigh of relief.

After Ellis had removed the alarm from the ceiling, he brought it over for her to see. The person hadn't removed the batteries but instead had cut the wires connecting the batteries to the alarm.

"Most of these units will squawk when you remove the batteries. By cutting the wires, they were able to stay silent," Ellis said.

"I didn't know that," Lydia said.

Ellis nodded. "Someone had some knowledge of how these things worked," he said. "That's another clue. Now, I just have to hope that whoever it was who stole the units from upstairs took them back to their place, and didn't just toss them."

"Right," Lydia said. Should she go looking in the trash receptacles up and down Main Street? Maybe later that afternoon. Or maybe Ellis would have to do it.

Next, Ellis went over to the stove and used more tape on the handles.

"Single fingerprint—probably a thumbprint—only on one side of these," he said, showing her the tape. "And I bet it's yours."

"There should be lots of fingerprints there," Lydia said. "Not just mine, but Misty's as well." It wasn't that they never cleaned the handles of the stove, but it didn't happen every day.

"Exactly," Ellis said. "The perpetrator cleaned up after themselves. We probably won't find any fingerprints anywhere, not even on the paper in the door jamb."

That was both good and bad. Good, because that it meant that Lydia had made the right call, asking Ellis to process the crime scene by himself.

Bad, because it meant whoever had tried to kill her and her guests had gone about it very methodically.

Lydia watched Ellis work. He moved slowly, documenting everything, first with photographs then with a sketch.

She found she enjoyed this, watching those big, gentle hands do their job. She'd heard the phrase, "competence porn" before. Watching him, she really understood the concept.

"You sleep down on this floor, don't you?" Ellis asked as he was finishing up.

"My bedroom is just past this wall," Lydia told him, pointing to the western wall of the kitchen.

"I'm surprised that you didn't succumb to the gas," Ellis said, peering at her closely.

"I did feel awful when I woke up. Had a headache and felt lethargic. But I always sleep with a window open," Lydia explained. "Oh! That probably eliminates Neil."

Ellis just turned and looked at her, one eyebrow raised.

Geez. She'd never been able to do that, had never been that cool. She remembered trying to teach herself that one-eyebrow trick when she'd been in high school, but had never been able to get her muscles to do that.

"Neil Roswell. My ex. He knows that I prefer to sleep that way." Lydia didn't add that she always slept in just a T-shirt as well. Ellis didn't need to know how she slept. He would have to discover that himself.

Ellis nodded, thinking. "All right. I'm going to go upstairs and examine the brackets, from where alarms were removed. Chances are I won't find anything, but I want to document them anyway." He looked around, then said formally, "I now release the kitchen back to you."

"Thank you," Lydia said, happy that he understood that she really needed to start cutting fruit for breakfast.

"I have a favor to ask," Ellis said slowly before Lydia could start work again. "Don't tell Misty Martìnez about this. Or anyone else, actually."

"She isn't a suspect, is she?" Lydia asked, surprised.

"No, but she is a gossip," Ellis said with a wry grin. "And once she knows, everyone in town will know. She has an amazing network of contacts. I'd like to keep this quiet for now, if that's possible."

"Good point," Lydia said. It pleased her that he'd been thinking of her reputation. Then again, maybe he had other reasons.

"You tell me if anything else is missing," he said as he picked up the stepstool.

Lydia had already pulled out the drawer with her knives in it. "Everything's here," she said after a moment. That had been her biggest fear—that whoever had turned on the gas was planning on killing again.

And this time, not implicating her with merely a letter opener.

After Ellis had left, Lydia scurried around the kitchen, trying to get everything set before guests started arriving. She quickly came up with a story for Misty about why the windows were open and she was so late—she'd slept in and still felt tired, and the fresh air was helping her wake up.

Still, Lydia couldn't help but wonder why Ellis didn't want her telling Misty. Or anyone else. Was he setting a trap?

She shivered again when she thought about how close of a call they'd all had. The explosion wouldn't have just killed her, but all of her guests. Including Ellis. Had that been the real reason why the killer had done this?

Once Ellis caught whoever it was, hopefully Lydia would have a chance to ask them.

But the person needed to be caught soon. Before they killed again.

When Misty came in about an hour later, she was bursting with news. "Neil's been spotted again, yesterday afternoon," she said. "Guadalupe, who runs the ice cream shop over near the post office? She saw Neil, even chatted with him for a few minutes. He said he was here to see his family."

Lydia peered at Misty, confused. "Neil doesn't eat ice cream. He has a dairy intolerance," she said slowly. "Or at least, that was what he'd always claimed."

He'd never actually gotten himself tested or anything. It was just one more thing she had to be careful of around him. Luckily, they'd found some amazing dairy-free butter as well as cheese so he could indulge himself sometimes. If she was being fair, she did remember how bad his stomach got the few times he did have dairy, how he'd have to run for the toilet. The over-the-counter pills he got for reducing lactic acid helped, but it was always better if he just avoided it.

"That is strange," Misty said. "But he gave Guadalupe that name when he ordered his ice cream. Neil Roswell."

Lydia shook her head. Of course, Neil would discover that

he could actually eat dairy after she'd left. Or maybe he'd found better pills. Being denied dairy for so long was part of the reason why she served cheese on so many things that she cooked now.

"Guadalupe promised to call if he showed up again," Misty said. She bustled around the counter and looked more carefully at Lydia. "Bad night?" she guessed.

"Yeah," Lydia said, relieved that there was a good opening for her lie, that she didn't have to find an excuse for explaining the gas and everything. "Didn't sleep well. Still have a headache." That, at least, wasn't a lie, though her head was feeling better.

"You want me to prep back here?" Misty asked.

"Sure," Lydia said, handing her the knife. She escaped into the restaurant. She hadn't realized until just then how nervous she'd been feeling in the kitchen, how uncomfortable she still was back there.

Damn it! Whoever had come and attacked her place was *not* going to win. She would be comfortable here. This was her home.

Nothing, and nobody, was going to drive her from it. Period.

20

———

*L*ydia had just put all the sheets into the dryer when Alice came in to work Sunday afternoon. Almost all the rooms were changing over. Lydia hadn't been lying when she'd said she was booked full—until Ellis left, she wouldn't have another open room until August.

"Hi, Lydia!" Alice said cheerfully as she walked in. "Mama said to be sure to tell you that I had a nightmare last night."

"Thank you for letting me know," Lydia said, looking up at Alice. The girl did have dark lines under her eyes, and her round face seemed puffy. She wore her usual navy blue polo with jean-shorts and sandals, her parents always dressing her to look like everyone else.

Alice had nightmares at least once or twice a month. They would keep her up for most of the night, and either her mother or her father would spend the time with her. It meant that she would be tired and grumpy the next day. Lydia tried to let Alice go home early those days.

But it also meant that Alice had an alibi for the previous night. Not that Lydia had even considered that Alice would have come in and turned on the gas as well as stolen the alarms. That much planning would have been far beyond her abilities.

Still, Lydia made a note to be sure to tell Ellis about it, so he would stop considering Alice as a suspect. Unless he believed that whoever had turned on the gas had not been the killer. Lydia still believed the two acts were done by the same person.

"Are you feeling better?" Lydia asked. At Alice's nod, Lydia added, "I had bad dreams too." It was close enough to the truth.

"You should take a nap," Alice proclaimed solemnly. Then she yawned.

"So should you," Lydia said, laughing. "Come on. Let's get the cleaning done quickly so we can both take some time off."

"All right," Alice said cheerfully, following Lydia up the stairs.

At least the smell of gas had dissipated quickly, and Lydia had been able to close up all the windows. She was tempted to leave one or two open that evening, just in case the attacker came back. But no, she couldn't do anything out of the ordinary. She had to act as if everything was the same.

It was the only way she could fight back right now, to reclaim her home.

Alice and Lydia had a good routine, and so the rooms were cleaned in short order. Lydia texted Jen McGowen, letting her know to get her daughter early. The pair of them sat in the restaurant after they were finished, talking about the picnic that Alice's family was planning on Wednesday.

"You should come!" Alice proclaimed again. "Mitch wants to see you."

"And why is that?" Lydia asked. She doubted that he was interested in her any more than she was interested in him.

"It's for his book," Alice said solemnly. "Wants to talk with you about the case."

"I see," Lydia said. "There isn't really much more to tell. The detective is working on it."

"I know!" Alice said. "I talked with him again yesterday."

"Did you?" Lydia said, her hackles rising. "What did you talk about?"

"The eggs," Alice said. "I was just collecting them, you know."

"Good," Lydia said, warmth suddenly filling her. She'd told Ellis that Alice had merely been collecting the eggs, that she hadn't been planning on using them on Schooner's house, not until the thought occurred to her that Friday.

Had it already been more than a week since the old man had been killed? It seemed like forever ago. Things wouldn't get back to normal, either, until the killer had been caught.

After Alice left, Lydia stayed sitting in the restaurant for a while. Should she maybe go take a nap? Before she could get up, Misty came into the room. "Guadalupe just called. Neil is there."

Lydia stood up. "Can she delay him?" It would take her fifteen to twenty minutes to walk to the ice cream shop from the B&B. Driving might or might not take just as long, depending on how many tourists were clogging the two main streets through town.

Just then, Lydia's phone buzzed. It was a text from Patrice.

Neil just came in.

"Wait a minute," Lydia said. Her chest suddenly felt tight, as if there weren't enough air. She turned to face Misty. "Is Neil still at Guadalupe's shop?"

"She just called," Misty confirmed. "He had just walked in."

Lydia showed Misty the text from Patrice. "How can he be in two places at once?"

"I don't know," Misty said. "But Guadalupe wouldn't have called if he weren't there."

"Does Guadalupe actually know Neil by sight?" Lydia asked.

"She'd seen pictures of him, at the high school, but she'd never met him before," Misty admitted. "She wasn't sure it was him, the first time she saw him, so she asked the guy his name. He told her that yes, he was Neil Roswell."

"I bet he isn't, not really. Patrice knows Neil," Lydia said. "She wouldn't be fooled." What was going on here?

Misty nodded. "I'll let Guadalupe know. Should she try to delay the guy?"

"No," Lydia said. "Though if she can get a picture of him, that might be useful for the cops later. But only if she can do it without him realizing it."

Lydia took off quickly, heading out the door, rushing up Main Street. She had to get to Patrice's bakery before the real Neil took off. She texted Patrice as she walked, asking her to delay her ex if at all possible.

Crap! Why were there so many tourists out today? She actually had to step into the street to get around the first group ambling down the sidewalk. A second large cluster were gathered at the cute window display of the little clothing boutique. Normally, Lydia would have been happy to see tourists interested in more than just restaurants and bars. Right now, she'd cheerfully strangle them all for getting in her way.

"He's gone," Patrice said as soon as Lydia walked in. "He said he was here visiting his family. Hadn't gone to see you. Seemed surprised that you were here."

"Really?" Lydia said. He'd known that she'd come back here just after the divorce.

Patrice nodded. "I told him that you'd opened a B&B just down the street. Told him he should stop by."

"Do you know where he might have gone next?" Lydia asked, opening the door again.

"Nope. He wasn't that talkative," Patrice said, grimacing. "Never knew what you saw in that guy."

Lydia snorted. "At this point, neither do I."

Lydia walked back out onto the street, looking up and down. The B&B was east of the bakery, further up along Main Street. As she hadn't seen Neil when she'd been walking this way, he had to have gone the other direction.

If he was walking at all. He might have just gotten into his car and driven off after stopping by the bakery. He liked driving. He'd never understood why Lydia preferred walking everywhere.

Still, Lydia headed up the street, away from the B&B, keeping a careful eye peeled for Neil. It had been five years since she'd last seen him. He probably wouldn't have changed that much.

She stopped in Janice's consignment store, in case Neil was hiding in the back, as well as Bob's hardware store just up the street. No one had seen Neil, though many of the shopkeepers didn't know who she was talking about. They'd come into town long after Lydia and Neil had graduated from high school.

Lydia kept looking, even stopping in at *The Cove*, though it wasn't the sort of establishment that would Neil go to. But only a few regulars sat in the big bar, the TVs all turned on and loudly displaying whatever game was being featured.

Finally, Lydia turned around, defeated, and started slowly walking back to her B&B. Neil was in town. She believed Patrice. However, someone was also impersonating Neil. Was that to throw suspicion for the murder onto him? He had hated Schooner Thomas. Blamed him for making it harder for him to get ahead.

After debating with herself for a few moments, Lydia turned and walked up Barton Avenue, heading toward the precinct. While she didn't have anything definitive, it was still an oddity—someone impersonating her ex—and she thought the detective should know about.

It wasn't that she just wanted to see Ellis again. Not at all.

21

The front of the police station looked the same as it had the last time Lydia had stopped in here, with beige walls, brown carpet, and that unmistakable décor that screamed "government agency." Sergeant Gonzales sat behind the desk on the right.

Huh. Seemed that the bright blue plush toy belonged to him. Somehow, Lydia had thought it was the other officer's. Had it been given to him by one of his kids?

"Can I help you?" the sergeant asked as Lydia came walking in.

"Is Detective Avery here?" Lydia asked. They hadn't given him a desk out here. Maybe he worked in a room in the back. Or maybe he was somewhere else, detecting.

The Sergeant considered her request for a moment. "What is this about?"

"I wanted to tell him about a strange occurrence," Lydia said.

Lydia regretted her words as soon as they left her mouth. She could tell that Sergeant Gonzales was trying to contain an eye roll. How many others had come in here, demanding to see the detective, with the same sort of flimsy excuse?

"Why don't you just tell me about it?" Sergeant Gonzales said. He smiled at her. Or at least he tried to. He wasn't a man who was comfortable with the softer side of his emotions, that was obvious.

"Can't I tell you both at once?" Lydia countered. "That way I won't have to repeat myself and I can get back to the B&B."

The Sergeant pressed his lips tightly together, giving him more of a thoughtful appearance instead of his usual scowl. He appeared to be weighing the eventual outcome. After all, Lydia could have waited until she saw the detective later on that evening at the B&B. That she'd come here might mean what she had to say was important.

"All right, let me see if he's available," the sergeant said eventually.

"Thank you," Lydia said, as she prepared to wait. She understood his careful wording left him with the option of coming back without the detective, in case Ellis decided he really was too busy to see her.

However, Lydia didn't have to wait for long, as both the sergeant and Ellis came walking out into the front of the station.

"What is it?" Ellis asked. He smiled at her, as if he was happy to see her. Not just a detective thing, but as a man.

Lydia was glad that she didn't blush, because that smile promised all sorts of danger.

"My ex, Neil Roswell, is in town," she said, nodding at Sergeant Gonzales. "Don't know if you remember him or not."

"Quarterback of the high school football team, wasn't he?" the sergeant said. "We won state that year, because of him," he said, explaining to Detective Avery.

"Yes, anyway," Lydia said, trying to move the conversation beyond Neil's glory days. She'd heard far too much about them. "He's been spotted in town. Both at Patrice's bakery, as well as at Guadalupe's ice cream shop. At the same time!"

The two men looked at each other. "I'm not sure I understand the significance," Ellis said.

"The person at the ice cream shop introduced himself as Neil Roswell to Guadalupe," Lydia said. "But Patrice knows Neil on sight. So how can he be in two places at once? Someone is impersonating him!"

"Why would they do that?" Ellis said.

"To throw suspicion on him!" Lydia said. "Isn't it obvious? The killer must be the second Neil!"

Ellis nodded. "I see," he said. "Did Neil have a grudge against Schooner Thomas?"

"Yes," Lydia said. "A big one. Schooner Thomas wouldn't write any letters of recommendation for Neil, for college. He didn't get into his first few college picks. He always blamed Schooner for that."

"When did you say he was first spotted?" Ellis asked, pulling a notebook out of his pocket.

"Last week," Lydia admitted.

"So before the murder," Sergeant Gonzales said.

"Yes," Lydia said slowly. "But it might not have been the real Neil. It might have been the imposter."

Both officers merely looked at her. Lydia could tell that at least the sergeant wanted to roll his eyes at her, possibly Ellis as well.

"He cannot be two places at once," Lydia insisted. She knew her ex. And he had absolutely no special abilities.

"You're right, that is an oddity," Ellis said eventually. "Thank you for bringing this to my attention."

Lydia knew she was being dismissed. Would anyone look

into it further? Probably not. She wanted to suggest that Sergeant Gonzales could go and interview Guadalupe while the detective went to see Patrice. But they obviously had more important things to do than to actually investigate.

"Fine," she said. She didn't storm out of the police department. Not quite.

Instead, she walked out like a woman with a mission.

The detective probably considered Neil a suspect. Or something stupid like that. But Lydia was *not* one of those idiotic women who lived with a serial killer for decades and never suspected a thing.

No, she was going to have to find the real Neil, then *prove* that the idiot didn't kill Schooner Thomas.

It was the only way to make sure she would be able to sleep at night.

*L*ydia tried to enjoy the warm sunshine outside as she stalked up and down the streets of downtown Lake Hope, searching for Neil. It only left her sweating more. Her stomach clenched as if she hadn't eaten anything, which, okay, maybe she'd kind of skipped eating because of gas and everything.

She found herself staring at any many who was the right height and had dark hair. Was that Neil? The guy holding hands with a much taller woman? Or the guy over there, walking with three other bros who all looked like wannabe hipsters?

Who was the imposter? Where was the real Neil?

Lydia nearly jumped out of her skin when her phone chimed. But it was just Misty texting her, letting her know that Guadalupe hadn't been able to get a picture. Nor had she been able to get a good look at the vehicle the imposter had been driving. She didn't think that he suspected her of not believing him, though. He'd promised to come by the next time she was open, which would be Tuesday, as she was closed Monday like many of the shops were.

Lydia constrained herself from stopping every male who bore a passing resemblance to Neil. She possibly freaked a few of them out, following them into or out of a shop until she could get a closer look.

Everyone seemed so happy and carefree. Lydia remembered feeling that way, once. Had it really only been a week since she'd learned of Schooner's death?

But someone was out there. Someone who had turned on all the gas at the B&B, intending to do both her and her guests harm.

Had the real target been the detective? Lydia couldn't be sure. Or had it just been to frighten her?

She was sure it hadn't been Neil. He wasn't that vindictive. Neil talked a good game. Very little moved him into action, though. Or as Patrice had once said, all hat and no cattle.

Slowly, Lydia wound her way back to the B&B. It would be time to greet the new guests coming in soon. Misty had Sunday afternoons off to spend time with her family, so it would be just Lydia. Misty, like Lydia, worked seven days a week during the busy seasons, though she only worked half days Sundays and Mondays, coming in after Lydia started and leaving after lunch.

For a moment, Lydia wondered if it had been Misty who'd killed Schooner Thomas, or turned on the gas. But she couldn't imagine why her co-worker would do such a thing.

Unless she was really a criminal mastermind, who just appeared to be friendly with everyone…

Lydia couldn't help but snort out loud. Misty was comfortable and kind. While all of her own children were grown, she had grandchildren as well as cousins and brothers and nephews and nieces and so on. She would have had to be a master manipulator to have hidden her true nature not just from Lydia but from everyone.

Shaking her head, Lydia finally got back to the B&B. The rooms were all cleaned and set. She could just hang out, maybe do some reading, while waiting for her guests to arrive.

Of course, someone was already waiting in the restaurant when she got there.

"Can I help you?" Lydia asked as she came in.

The tall stranger turned. Lydia felt her entire world shake loose, then right itself again.

"Hello, Lydia."

"Hello, Neil."

22

———

*L*ydia critically studied her ex. It had been five years since she'd seen him.

Neil was dressed nicely, as usual. While Ed and Alan had never liked Neil as a person, they did have to admit that he dressed well most of the time. His black T-shirt didn't have a logo on it, as he found it morally offensive to be a walking advertisement for anyone (other than himself). He'd maintained all of his hair, as well as his athletic physique, probably with the same amount of complaining and whining as he'd done when she'd been around. His muscular legs looked good in the tan shorts he wore. She remembered joking with him about how he had better knees than she did, and how he should have been the one in skirts. Even his black athletic shoes looked good, more like a millionaire slumming rather than an MBA on vacation.

He was only three months younger than she—they'd shared jokes about her being the "older woman" while he'd been a "boy toy." He looked younger than her as well, people frequently guessing him to be five to ten years younger than he actually was. However, she could see that gray had finally touched his dark hair, right at the temples. Of course, that would just make him look more distinguished, not old. Unlike the few gray hairs that streaked her own head.

"How are you?" Neil asked after a few moments, obviously taking the time to study her as well.

Lydia bet that he wasn't actually impressed by what he saw. She wore her usual braid with the wisps pinned back, a raspberry-sherbet colored T-shirt, light gray shorts and sandals. She hadn't gained any weight—she was far too busy cleaning other people's toilets, as it were. But she had gained wrinkles.

"I'm good," Lydia said. "How are you?"

Neil nodded. "About the same," he said eventually. "So, this is your place?"

"It is," Lydia said. She tried not to be defensive, but instead, to show him just how proud she was. She had her own B&B. She was her own boss. Sure, she worked a lot of hours, but she enjoyed her life, overall.

The dining room was clean, all the mugs, plates, and silverware put away behind the counter, ready for service Monday morning. The chairs and tables weren't carefully spaced across the floor yet. Later that evening, after her guests had checked in, she'd move all the tables out of the way and mop the floors. Then she'd set everything just so and have a fresh start at the beginning of the week.

It was a place she was proud of. She didn't care what Neil said or thought.

"Huh," was Neil's only comment. Then he turned his eye back to her. "You're looking good."

Was he surprised as how well she'd done while he wasn't in her life?

"Thank you," she said. "You too." She paused, and then, because she couldn't help herself, she had to ask, "So what are you doing here? You hate Lake Hope. Said you were never coming back."

"I didn't say that," Neil said, sounding defensive.

Lydia rolled her eyes and didn't reply. She wasn't about to get into that old argument with Neil. She'd threatened to record him on more than one occasion, particularly when he denied having said something that she clearly remembered him saying.

She waited, patiently. She was more than willing to wait him out.

When had she developed such patience? She was actually comfortable in the silence that grew between them. Was this part of maturing? She hadn't expected or realized it before now.

Finally, Neil replied. "My mom and dad are selling their place. They wanted me to come back and sort out the stuff I'd left here."

"I didn't think you'd left anything here that you'd value," Lydia said, confused. Was he lying? He'd made that claim more than once before as well.

"*They* were convinced that I had," Neil said with an eyeroll. "You know how they are."

Lydia actually didn't. She and Neil had never spent that much time with his parents either before or after they'd gotten married. She'd heard Neil's stories about them, but had quickly realized that when it came to Neil, she was only ever getting a single viewpoint on any event. Other people frequently had radically different viewpoints from his. Particularly her own.

"That can't be the only reason you came back," Lydia said after a moment, still probing for the truth.

"Maybe I wanted to check up on you, see how you were doing," Neil said.

"You didn't even know I was still in town," Lydia pointed out.

"You've already talked with Patrice," Neil said, laughing.

Well, that was new. Lydia felt herself standing up straighter. Normally, Neil would have been pissed off about Lydia challenging one of his stories. Not laughing.

"True," Lydia said slowly, not wanting to ask about the imposter just yet. Or possibly ever.

"I could never pull a fast one on you," Neil said after a few moments. "No matter how hard I tried. I never had anyone stand up to me like that."

"What, do you miss it?" Lydia asked, letting the sarcasm drip from her words. She crossed her arms over her chest. Their biggest fights had been over Neil's version of reality versus what had really happened.

"I do, actually," Neil said with what Lydia had always called his cute boy smile, the one that, at least in the past, had melted her heart.

Fortunately, it didn't appear to have the same effect that it had once had. Instead, Lydia felt herself growing angry. Neil always did that to her, made her rage like no one else.

"I call bull hockey," Lydia said, not bothering to hide the heat behind her words. "You don't really miss it. Or me."

Instead of instantly replying, Neil paused to study her again for a few moments.

"No, I actually do," he said more soberly. "I didn't realize it at the time, but I kind of need someone to keep me in line."

Lydia had never even imagined those words coming out of Neil's mouth. She felt her own mouth open and shut a couple of times.

"You're kidding me," she finally said, shaking her head. She shifted uncomfortably from one foot to the other. She tightened her arms across her chest, as if hugging herself.

What would she have done if he'd come to her and said those things right after the divorce had been finalized? Would she have changed her mind and gone back to him?

Neil laughed softly. "We all grow up, at some point."

Lydia could *not* deal with that right now. Couldn't even consider that Neil might want to be part of her life again. That was even more unsettling than finding out that a killer lived among them in her town, or finding the gas on that morning.

"When did you get in?" Lydia asked, deliberately changing the subject.

Neil nodded, as if he understood what a bombshell he'd just laid on her. "Last week," he said.

"When, exactly?" Lydia said, trying to nail down his timeline. She knew he hadn't killed Schooner. But still…

"Came out a week ago Friday," Neil said. "Was here for the weekend, then headed back to Seattle. Came back this weekend to finish up."

Damn it! That meant he could have killed Schooner.

"Peter, one of the owners of Blue Pond winery, thought he saw you on Thursday," Lydia said. She'd double checked with Bill when exactly he'd thought he'd seen Neil.

"Why would I stop at a winery?" Neil said, confused. "I didn't leave Seattle until Friday, after work. You know I'm not a wine drinker."

That made sense to Lydia. Blue Pond was out in the middle of nowhere. Had Peter seen the imposter instead? Plus, Neil liked his beer with the boys. He only drank wine when he thought it made the right impression.

Though whoever had stopped at the vineyard had asked if they had any beer…

"Did you know that Schooner Thomas was killed?" Lydia said, hoping to surprise him.

Neil gave her a big grin. "Yup. Been looking forward to pissing on the old man's grave."

"The police still don't know who murdered him," Lydia said. "Any stranger coming into town is going to be a suspect."

"I didn't kill him," Neil said. He looked offended.

Lydia studied him closely. She didn't think he was lying. But how could she be certain? Neil certainly had changed a lot in the past five years.

"The police will still want to talk with you," she said.

Neil nodded. Lydia could easily read his expression as, "Bring it." He was ready to take on the world, as always.

"Where were you this past Saturday night?" Lydia said.

"What is with the third degree?" Neil said. He shook his head, but responded anyway. "Came into town late. Was at a Mariners' game. Great seats along the third base line. I have a bunch of witnesses as well."

That actually didn't help his case, at least as far as Lydia was concerned. He could have come to the B&B when he'd gotten into town and turned on the gas.

Except that he hadn't even realized that this was her place.

Were the two not connected?

That still didn't answer who was impersonating Neil, or why they'd tried to implicate her in Schooner's death by stabbing him with one of her letter openers.

The bell hanging above the lintel rang as someone came in. "Hi!" Lydia said, turning and smiling at them.

"Hi." It was an older couple who Lydia vaguely recognized. "We're the Hendricks," the gentleman announced proudly.

"Right!" Lydia said. They'd stayed with her every year right around this time. She turned back to Neil. "I need to take care of my guests, now," she explained. "Can you come back here later tonight? Say, after eight?"

Neil shook his head. "Sorry. Can't. Have dinner with the folks. I'll be here until Tuesday though. Lunch tomorrow?"

Lydia so wanted to say yes. However, she knew that Theo would kill her if she did. And while Neil was her ex, Theo was still her brother. "Late dinner?" she countered.

"Sure," Neil said. "I'll stop by at seven."

Lydia blinked, surprised that Neil was being so accommodating. Was it because he had an audience? Or had he actually changed?

"See you then," she said, turning away from him and firmly toward the Hendricks.

A look of anger crossed Neil's face so quickly Lydia wasn't sure if she imagined it or not. Was he angry at being dismissed? Had he expected a kiss goodbye? Or some kind parting words?

Too bad. She wasn't a teenager, and no longer his wife. She had guests to attend to.

Neil let himself out of the B&B and Lydia easily fell into the role of gracious hostess.

She would deal with Neil later, as well as process all the implications and nuances of their conversation, that night, alone in her rooms.

---

*L*ydia checked, re-checked, then triple-checked the front door, the back door, and the windows. She'd special ordered new carbon monoxide alarms, having them shipped tomorrow, instead of contacting Danny and asking him for more. Not that she thought he was a suspect, but she didn't want anyone to know what had happened.

Nothing seemed amiss. Lydia wasn't sure what she needed to do in order to help herself feel more safe. Give herself time, more than anything else, she suspected.

Finally, she made her way back to her rooms. She poured herself the last glass of the really good chardonnay that Bill had left her, but then let it sit on her side table as she curled up in the wingback chair in her living room. She only had two rooms back here—the bedroom and the living room—as well as a small pantry where she kept some of her own supplies, a microwave and a small, apartment-sized refrigerator.

As with her bedroom, Lydia had made every design decision based on whether the outcome would delight her. She had two comfy chairs that she loved curling up in, one a wingback done in a rich green, gold, and red fabric, the other broader and wider, done in a soft green fabric, with wooden arms and brass accents. She also had a loveseat that was a dark purple micro-suede that was the perfect size for when she wanted to curl up and nap, though most of the time she didn't. The window over the loveseat didn't have much of a view, so she had a beautiful white lace shade drawn over it instead.

The ceiling in here was the same warm cedar wood as in the bedroom. She didn't have an overhead light, but instead, several beautiful lamps that she could control from the light switch near the door. The rugs were thick and warm across the dark hardwood, so she could go barefoot when she wanted to. She had a TV hanging on one wall, where it was easy to watch from the loveseat, not that she turned it on that often. While she had a few books on the shelves in the corner, she preferred reading on her ebook reader. She was always in the middle of several books at the same time, and would read whichever one struck her fancy in the evening.

The only sound was the quiet hum of the fridge from the

pantry, along with the occasional car passing down the street. As her rooms were behind the building, she didn't have anyone walking around above her. The air was cooler back here, deliberately so, but not so cold that she needed to put on a sweater that night.

It was a self-contained existence. She knew that. While she did have enough space for a few friends to come over, for the most part, she spent her time here alone. It suited her, particularly after she'd had to spend a lot of time dealing with guests and other people.

Tonight, her place felt more closed in than usual. Not that that was a bad thing. She wanted to draw her rooms in around her and over her head, like a blanket of protective armor.

She was safe here. At least tonight. She took a sip of her wine and let the mellow chardonnay wash over her tongue, trying to find the hints of walnuts and butter that Bill claimed. After taking a deep breath, she settled back more firmly in her chair, trying to make herself relax, unclench that knot in the center of her chest.

So Neil was back. And possibly wanted to make a play to get back into her life. She'd been talking with someone else when Detective Avery had gone through the restaurant. He'd nodded in her direction, but then gone upstairs to his room, so she hadn't had a chance to talk with him, to let him know that she'd found the real Neil.

Let the detective do his own damned investigating.

What was she going to do? She didn't know if Ellis was even interested, though she suspected he was. Like her, though, he probably didn't want a long-distance relationship.

And what about Neil? They'd had some good times, even with the fights and his lying. Did she want that back in her life?

What if he was the killer? What would that say about her, not suspecting him before?

No. He couldn't have done it. That said too much about her, not him.

In the quiet of the night, all alone in her room, Lydia could admit to being a smidge lonely. For the most part she was fine, satisfied with her situation and being on her own. If her parents had been here, she might have gone to see them. But she had good friends, a good job, a good life.

A partner would have made everything richer. She could admit that.

Maybe some year someone would move to town and she'd be able to have a relationship. A normal, adult relationship. Not someone she'd have to fight to "keep in line." Really, Neil just needed to grow up and handle himself. And not with someone who would freeze her out like Ellis probably would do on a regular basis, when he switched from being a man to being a detective.

Nope. Lydia needed—deserved—someone better.

She just had to be patient until they came along.

heo was on time, and as dorky looking as always, with black sandals, skinny gray pants, and a faded red T-shirt that didn't do him any favors—looking like a hand-me-down from a much larger brother.

"Hi," Lydia said, greeting him as he came in. She'd already taken off her apron and had been wiping down the counter at the back of the restaurant. They had closed early that day. Not that many customers had shown up for lunch. She walked around the counter and came to stand beside him.

"What, you're ready?" Theo asked, obviously surprised.

"I even remembered you were coming and everything," Lydia snarked.

Theo just snorted at her and led her back out the door, into the street. The day had dawned warm and stayed hot. Even the lake breeze wouldn't be able to keep the town cool. It was the true start of summer. Lydia found herself sweating far too quickly. She was glad she was in her navy blue shorts and off-white T-shirt. Not that she would have dressed any differently, no matter who might be looking at her, like Neil or Ellis.

"Do you like tacos?" Lydia asked as she walked beside her brother. She thought he did, but she didn't want to presume.

"Yeah," Theo said. "Where we going?"

"Max's," Lydia explained. "The menu isn't extensive—he only serves tacos, burritos, and enchiladas. He used to run a food truck before he found the space to rent. But all of it is really tasty."

"Good," Theo said. "Sounds great. I heard from the 'rents this morning."

"Where are they?" She hadn't heard from them since they'd left. Honestly, she wasn't expecting much more than a couple of post cards, though they'd promised to call. If they remembered even that.

"North Dakota," Theo said. "Black Hills. They're having a blast."

"Huh," Lydia said. "Was that it? All they wanted?"

Theo gave her a wry grin. "Seemed they were checking up on me. Making sure that I hadn't turned into a hermit and that you were actually talking with me."

"Did you tell them about the wine tasting?" Lydia asked. She wanted to look good to her parents, as always.

"Nope. Told them I hadn't left the property since I'd arrived. I had all the shades drawn, the lights turned off, and had turned the house into a cave," Theo said.

"What?" Lydia said. "Why would you say that?" Her parents would kill her for not looking after her little brother. Damn it. She wasn't thirteen anymore. But this entire situation made her feel that way.

"I'm joking, I'm joking," Theo assured her. "You're too serious, like you've always been. You need to lighten up some."

Lydia sighed and shrugged. She couldn't yell at Theo as

much as she might want to. He was just being a bratty little brother, who didn't understand that she had far too much on her mind to "chill."

"I'm glad they're having a good time," Lydia said eventually, as they passed a couple of tourists on the sidewalk.

"Yeah, they really like the RV they've rented. May actually get one for themselves," Theo said. "Mom needed something to do. Hopefully sightseeing will fill the ticket for a while. She's spending so much time researching every place they're going."

"Of course she is," Lydia said with a grin. Then she sighed. She worried about her mom.

"I've wondered if there was some sort of volunteer organization that she could be part of now that she's no longer working," Lydia said. "The researching will only carry her for so long."

"I am not about to point her at a political campaign, though you and I both know that's exactly the sort of thing she'd thrive at," Theo said.

"Naw, she knows where all the dead bodies are," Lydia said. "None of the rich folk around here would support her."

"Not unless she stooped to blackmail," Theo said, grinning.

"True," Lydia said.

They walked for a little while. Though Lydia was glad for the chance to be outside, it was already getting too warm for her. They stuck to the shady side of the street as they walked, as did most of the tourists in the area. The blacktop of the street shimmered, and that thick smell of tar filled the air. Lydia noted that Bill's Boutique was having a sale. She'd have to remember to stop by later and pick up fliers for the B&B if it was going to last more than a week.

"Mom might actually decide to go into politics, though.

If she set her mind to helping a candidate," Lydia said after a few moments.

Theo laughed at her. "Don't you think that she's had enough of being the power behind the throne? I bet she runs herself."

"That…that…" Lydia didn't even know how to complete her sentence. It would be completely like her mother. And completely terrifying at the same time.

"Yup, that about sums it up," Theo agreed.

Lydia held open the door to the café for him, then followed him into the brightly lit space. The air was blessedly cool. It smelled of heavily-spiced meat and caramelized onions. She found her mouth watering as she walked up to the counter, Max wasn't there, but his brother was. They looked very similar: heavy-set Mexican men with round faces, reddened skin, and black hair that looked like it had been cut by someone putting a bowl on their heads then trimming all the hair that stuck out underneath.

After Lydia and Theo had ordered—fish tacos for her, chorizo burrito for him—they took their drinks out to the patio on the side of the building. A fan blew misted water at them, making them both feel instantly cooler. The smell of lovely greasy fried food that wasn't good for you carried through the air. They sat on hard metal chairs, as Lydia knew from past experience that the ones made from plastic would stick to her skin uncomfortably.

After a few moments of quiet, Theo looked at Lydia and said, "I don't remember you having this much patience, before."

Lydia shrugged, and said, "I probably didn't." She'd noticed it recently as well.

"It's nice," Theo said. He breathed out a sigh. "I feel as though I could relax around you. Maybe."

"Hopefully that's a good thing," Lydia said. She wasn't

sure how she felt around Theo yet. He seemed less thin that day, a little less hollowed out. Maybe being here was good for him, filling him back up.

"Maybe. Maybe not," Theo said after a few moments. He took another deep breath.

"Look, whatever dark secret you're holding, you don't actually have to tell me," Lydia said after a few more moments. "You have your own life, now. We both had issues when we were teens. Drama. What have you."

Theo nodded. "I've had to explain this to the detective already," he said after a few moments. "And Patrice knows. So I figured I could finally tell my sister."

"You look like you're going to throw up," Lydia volunteered after he didn't say anything immediately. He'd grown pale sitting there.

Theo grimaced at her. "Thanks," he said. "Look. I don't know how to say this. So I'm just going to say words and you're going to have to listen and not interrupt. Okay?"

Lydia nodded, intrigued but also worried.

"I did some experimenting when I was in high school," Theo said after a couple more deep breaths.

"Drugs?" Lydia said, unable to contain herself.

Theo glared at her.

Lydia pressed her lips together, chagrined. She mimed locking her lips and throwing away the key. She wouldn't speak again until he said that she could. She could contain herself. Really.

"No. With boys. My age," Theo finally admitted.

Lydia furrowed her brow at him but remained silent, despite the numerous questions that flooded through her. Was her brother gay? Bi? Did it matter?

"Principal Thomas caught Ernie Santos and me once, in the locker room," Theo said.

Theo turned even whiter. He looked as though he was

having a hard time taking in air. Lydia reached across the table and squeezed his hand, giving him an encouraging smile. She still didn't know what to think, but she understood how difficult this must be for him.

"Thanks," Theo said after a few moments, letting go of her hand. "The asshole told us we were going to hell. Told us that we were such a huge disappointment, not just to our parents but to society. Threatened to expose us to the entire school, as well as any potential employer."

Lydia nodded, taking a deep breath through her nose so she wouldn't say anything. What an awful thing for anyone to say to a young boy still trying to figure out his life.

"Ernie's sister told Patrice, who came to talk to me the next day," Theo said. He gave Lydia a weak smile. "Wanted me to know that she supported me, would stand by me, was still my friend, regardless of what that asshole Thomas might say."

"Can I say something?" Lydia said. She really, really wanted to tell Theo that she supported him as well.

"Not yet," Theo said. "See, her coming to me just confused me more. Because I still liked her. I mean, *like* liked her."

Lydia blinked. She was sure her confusion was obvious.

"So I liked Patrice. And I liked Ernie. And there were others I was attracted to," Theo said quietly. "I knew the term bisexual, but, I mean, I was straight, right? I still liked girls. I only played with boys. It wasn't the same."

Lydia nodded, saddened. They'd grown up in a small town in Central Washington. Many, perhaps most, of the people who still lived there would consider Theo an abomination.

"Anyway, after that, I stopped looking at boys. Was only going to be attracted to women. And I was mostly successful," Theo said. "Then Steve came along."

Lydia kept her word and stayed silent, nodding again, encouraging Theo to keep talking. Who knew that he had such depths?

It made sense to her now, though, why he had refused to go with her to visit Ed and Alan in New York, why he'd always seemed so resentful of them. They hadn't necessarily been out—it had been the late '90s, and it still wasn't easy for anyone to live an alternative lifestyle. However, they did live together as "roommates," an open secret of their real relationship as they had only the one bedroom.

They would have been too much for a confused bisexual boy to handle, particularly one afraid of who he was and how he felt.

"Steve didn't come into the picture until after Jasmine and I were divorced," Theo assured Lydia. "But he's kind of here, part of my life, now."

"Can I say anything yet?" Lydia asked again.

Theo nodded.

"Is Steve here? In Lake Hope?" she said.

Theo shook his head. "No, he's waiting for me back in Spokane. Waiting for me to make up my mind. Figure out what I really want."

"Sorting out some things, huh?" Lydia said, trying to gently tease.

Theo nodded and shot her a smile.

"Do you love him?" Lydia said after a moment.

Theo sighed. "How do you really know when you're in love with someone? I thought I was in love with Jasmine."

"And maybe you were, at one point," Lydia said. "But people change. And sometimes they fall out of love."

"I don't want that to happen with Steve," Theo said softly.

"Then don't let it happen," Lydia said. "Though I'm probably the last one you want advice from. Look at me."

"No one expected you to stay married to that asshole," Theo assured her.

"Thanks, I think," Lydia said dryly.

"Seriously. No one wanted you to stay with him," Theo said.

"You know he's back in town," Lydia said. "We're going out to dinner later tonight."

"What?" Theo asked. "You know he hated Principal Thomas, too. Probably more than I did. I remember him ranting about it."

"Yeah, but I don't think he killed the man," Lydia said. "That would have called for actual follow-through on his part. And he always talked a much better game than he played."

"True," Theo said. After a few moments, he cautiously asked, "So, what do you think?"

"I don't know," Lydia said truthfully. "I want you to be happy." It surprised her, but the words were accurate. She did wish her brother happiness.

"Steve makes me happy," Theo said after a few moments. He sighed. "Jasmine and her family will never understand, though."

Lydia snorted at him. "I call bull hockey. Don't you remember Jasmine's uncle Nik? He was at your wedding."

"Uhmmm, maybe?" Theo said. "Wait. I do. You're right!"

"They might not understand that you like both men and women," Lydia said. "But honestly, who cares? You get to like or love whoever you want these days."

"Even in a small town like Spokane?" Theo asked.

"Even here in Lake Hope," Lydia replied. "And a pox on anyone who would stop you. Particularly some asshole like Schooner Thomas."

"I had planned on confronting him, you know," Theo

said after a few moments. "Telling him that he was wrong. I did find happiness. And I'm going to find more."

"Which is why the police think you're a suspect," Lydia guessed. "Because you were seen going to his house."

"Exactly," Theo said. He sighed. "Bad luck that it happened to be Friday night. I never got up the courage to actually knock on his door, though I had intended to."

"Probably a good thing that you didn't," Lydia said. "You might have disturbed the killer."

"I know," Theo said. "Believe me, I've thought of that. I just can't convince the police that it wasn't me, though."

"Then we'll have to figure out who did kill Schooner Thomas," Lydia said. "Before it's too late."

24

———

ydia found herself actually looking forward to meeting with Neil for dinner. Like Theo, she felt the need to see what was actually there, in front of her, versus all her memories.

She was aware that she'd never get back together with him. There was just too much water under that bridge. However, it wouldn't hurt to at least look at her options for a night, right?

For once, Lydia let her hair down, literally. She undid the braid she usually wore, letting her long hair flow down her back, to midway between her shoulder blades and her waist. She regularly got the ends trimmed, but it continued to grow longer. She used the fancy hairpins to hold back the wisps around her face, the ones with pretty pink and red rhinestones. Instead of a usual T-shirt, she wore a nicer, black-and-white polka-dot sleeveless blouse, that showed off her muscles as well as her figure, with a plain gray skirt and her nicer sandals. She didn't have any perfume, but she did add mascara to make her eyes bigger, as well as just a touch of pink lipstick.

She even twirled once in front of her mirror, knowing that Ed and Alan would have approved. While she would never look as casually fabulous as Patrice, she still managed a quiet, chic elegance.

And if Neil didn't appreciate that, well, he could just go right back to Seattle and leave her and her hometown alone.

Neil showed up ten minutes late, as usual. He would bitch loudly enough if someone else showed up late, but he was never on time himself. Lydia stood in the restaurant chatting with the Hendricks about their day's adventures at the various wineries.

"My dinner date is here," Lydia said, excusing herself and walking over to see Neil. She knew the speculation that the older couple were likely to have. She didn't care. She'd inured herself to her guests' gossip long ago.

Neil looked really good, actually, in a light blue-and-white striped shirt and navy blue pants, loafers and no socks. He filled out the shirt well, and she suspected that his butt was still rock solid.

"Shall we?" she asked as she walked over to where he was standing just inside the door.

"We shall," he said solemnly, holding the door open for her. His silver Audi was just outside.

"Where are we going?" Lydia asked as she slid into the car she remembered well. The seat curved around her, both supportive and comfortable. Neil had always taken good care of his car, the leather seats still supple and like new. No dirt marred the freshly vacuumed carpet, the dashboard was free of dust. It smelled faintly of the lemon leather cleaner he always used.

As always, the spotless condition of the car made Lydia want to put her feet up on the dash, just because.

"I thought we could go to *Palmer's*," Neil said.

"Splashing out?" Lydia said. She hadn't been to *Palmer's*

in years, though she frequently told honeymooners to go there. It was one of the fanciest restaurants in town. It was on Lake Hope itself, with beautiful views and an extensive deck. It catered to the rich folk who lived on the northern end of the lake, as well as to tourists who came to have one really good meal while on vacation.

Neil shrugged and started the car up. The engine purred as always. "Figured why not," he said. "It does have the best wine list of any of the restaurants."

Lydia rolled her eyes. "Since when did you care about fine wine?"

He grinned at her. "See? That's something I've missed."

Lydia kept her snort to herself.

Neil continued. "I figured that you would have developed a fine palate since you've been back, surrounded by good wine all the time, that you'd appreciate it."

"Okay," Lydia said. He may have even been telling her the truth—that he'd thought of her and her needs at some point when it came to this evening.

Probably, though, he had just wanted to try to impress her.

They chatted easily about Neil's work, catching up on some of the news about friends who Lydia hadn't seen in the last five years as they wound their way along the scenic lakeshore and up to the restaurant.

Palmer's still had the same elegance that Lydia remembered—low lights and heavy, leather furniture, with small intimate tables lit by candlelight. The heavenly smell of freshly baked bread filled the air, underlaid with scents of garlic and seared meat. Lydia found her stomach clamoring to be filled as they were shown to their seats. The maître d' unfolded the heavy cloth napkins and set them in their laps before handing them the large, stiff menus.

"Wow," Lydia said, looking it over. While the menu items hadn't changed much from the last time she'd been here, the prices had certainly increased to Seattle standards and beyond.

"I know, right?" Neil said. "It all looks amazing."

Lydia nodded, glad that he'd misinterpreted her exclamation, that he'd assumed she was just looking at the items available.

Neil handed her the wine list, saying, "You should pick us out a bottle that will go well with steak. That is, I'm assuming you want steak, right?"

"I do," Lydia said. She'd heard often enough from guests that the ribeye at *Palmer's* was amazing. They actually would serve it blue, which not many restaurants knew how to do. In addition, at least according to what she'd heard, they knew how to cook their other steaks perfectly.

After they'd ordered, Neil asked, "So tell me how you got into the B&B business."

"It started off almost as a lark," Lydia said. "I'd come back here after the divorce, wanting to take a little time to figure out what I wanted to do with my life."

Neil nodded. That much he already knew.

"So Dad and I were walking downtown and saw the For Sale sign on the old place," Lydia said. "I joked with him about how I should just buy that place and set myself up in business there. He didn't laugh, though. He just told me I could do anything I wanted to."

Lydia drew in a deep breath. She hadn't realized until just then how much the quiet, unwavering support of her parents, particularly her father, had meant to her.

"I kept thinking about it, though I hadn't been serious at the time," Lydia continued. "I took a tour of the building and found out how much they were asking for, then I got estimates for how much it would cost to do all the upgrades that needed doing. Figured out I could swing it if I did a lot of the work myself. I was sure my dad would help, as he'd retired recently. He works as a handyman now, when he wants to work."

Neil pressed his lips together, and Lydia would swear that he was just about to roll his eyes. "What?" she asked defensively.

"You got it all planned out, to the smallest detail, before you told anyone, didn't you?" he said.

"I did," Lydia said defensively.

She knew that she and Neil had argued about that in the past. But really, there wasn't anyone else in her life at that point. No one who needed to be involved with that decision.

"So you bought the place," Neil said.

"Yup. Spent about eight weeks fixing it up, adding on the laundry room, my personal rooms, and like that. Opened on August first. Had my first guest inquire about a room six nights after that. Was full for the first time by the end of August. And it's been going really well ever since," Lydia said, her voice full of pride.

The wine arrived just then, as well as the bread. Neil had the waiter show Lydia the bottle. He'd done that before, so it wasn't a complete change of behavior. She took a taste and immediately approved it. It was a Barbados, a lighter red, sweeter at the front with the perfect amount of acidity that would go well with their meal.

"Cheers," Neil said, clinking glasses with her.

"Cheers," Lydia said. Their usual toast had always been, "To better times," or "To even better times." She appreciated that Neil was stepping cautiously around their past.

Or maybe he'd just forgotten.

Lydia continued to talk, telling him about funny things

her guests had done, bringing him up to date on the gossip in town. He told her about his parents, his co-workers, his gym friends.

They were even able to share some jokes and were laughing when Neil suddenly stiffened.

"What is it?" Lydia asked, watching Neil pull back into himself.

"Seems my rival has just shown up," he said, gesturing with his wine glass over Lydia's shoulder.

"Your rival?" Lydia said, confused. She glanced over her shoulder.

Detective Avery was being shown to a table. He obviously appeared to be eating alone.

But why should Neil consider him a rival? Had she said anything about him while they'd been chatting? Maybe. And maybe more than she should have.

"Shouldn't we invite him over?" Lydia said, teasingly. It was more to bother Neil than because she really wanted to see Avery again. Really.

"No, we should not," Neil said. He looked displeased, as if those last bites of truly divine steak were now turning bitter in his mouth.

"You're right, we're nearly finished," Lydia said. She wasn't upset with herself for not insisting—this really was a night for her and Neil.

They had already ordered the apple cobbler and coffee to finish off their meal, though Lydia doubted she'd be able to eat more than a few bites of anything more. At least she had thought to cut the ribeye in half before she'd started eating, so she was going to have tasty leftovers later that week.

"Do you want to go out and have a nightcap after this?" Neil said.

Lydia realized that the moment of truth was at hand. She

thought for a moment, then just said the words that came to her.

No one would ever accuse her of being too sly.

"While I'm very glad to see you, and to realize that we can be friendly to each other, there isn't anything more for us," Lydia said.

Why had those words been so difficult to say? She didn't feel breathless, as if she was anxious or excited. No, she felt heavy and sad.

Maybe even though she'd always known that getting back together with Neil was a dream, it was hard to finally kill that fantasy all the way dead.

Neil sighed, but then he nodded. "I think you're right," he said slowly. "I had thought…well, never mind what I thought. I need someone like you in my life. Just…not you."

The words hurt more than Lydia had expected them to.

They also lightened her heart.

She and Neil were both free, at least of each other.

"Friends?" Lydia asked after taking another sip of her wine.

"Friends, at the very least," Neil said. He stuck his hand across the table and Lydia shook it.

"Good," Lydia said. "Because I'd hate to have to clear your name if we weren't. I'd do it anyway, though."

Neil nodded and smiled at her. "You always did go for fair, if nothing else."

Lydia wasn't exactly sure what Neil meant, but she would take it for now.

After the extremely delicious cobbler with fresh apples and heavy cream was served, Lydia found herself studying Neil across the table.

He would always be her ex. But maybe they could play up the fact that they were exes, still…

"What?" Neil asked, sounding defensive.

"I have a plan to catch whoever it is who's been impersonating you," Lydia said. "And hopefully, the killer."

Neil gave her a broad smile, the one that she always read with the words, "Bring it" tacked on in big broad letters.

This time, she really would.

---

25

*L*ydia complained loudly and bitterly to anyone who would listen about how awful her "date" with Neil had been the night before. She was sure she'd only have to mention it to Misty for everyone in town to hear, but Lydia felt like playing it up.

However, she felt as though she only had the one chance to catch whoever it was who was impersonating him.

Hopefully the news of their "date" would reach the killer's ears before he went for ice cream that afternoon. It was a small town, after all.

Alice had cheerfully come in on her day off to help clean the B&B that afternoon so Lydia could leave early and get a table at the coffee shop just across the street from Guadalupe's ice cream shop. She regretted her choice after just a few minutes—the afternoon was uncomfortably hot, the temperature in the upper nineties. If there had been a breeze from the lake, it might have been bearable, but the air was completely still. The blue of the sky had even paled, and waves of heat rose off the new asphalt. The smell of tar choked her throat.

At least Lydia had an iced coffee to drink, though she suspected the ice wasn't going to last for long. And she was wearing shorts, sandals, and a light-enough lavender T-shirt. Her braided hair hung heavy down the middle of her back. Maybe someday she'd get it all shorn off…

According to Guadalupe, the imitation Neil came into the shop around three PM. Lydia had arrived at the coffee shop just after two-thirty.

Luckily, she didn't have to wait too long. A beat-up old sports coupe pulled up and a tall, dark-haired, well-dressed man climbed out of it. The two were incongruous—someone wearing that nice of an outfit should be driving something other than a dinged up, rusted out old car.

It had to be the imposter. From across the street, Lydia could see the resemblance to Neil. She certainly would have stopped to look at the man twice when she'd been on her hunt for the real Neil, before he'd just shown up.

The man paused, peering up and down the street before he entered the ice cream shop. Lydia pretended to be very interested in the label on the side of her coffee cup for a few moments, breathing a sigh of relief when the imposter actually did go into the shop.

Gathering up her courage, Lydia stood up. She was going to get to the bottom of this, once and for all.

Lydia's heart pounded hard as she walked across the street. The coffee she'd drunk churned in her stomach. She blamed her suddenly sweating palms on the high temperature. The door handle felt cool against her skin.

Taking one more deep breath, Lydia pulled the door open and walked in. The man stood at the counter, talking with Guadalupe. He laughed, and Lydia heard the similarities to Neil's laugh.

So the imposter could sound like Neil as well.

Lydia waited next to the door while Guadalupe served

the imposter a cup of ice cream with hot fudge. She caught Lydia's eye and nodded, acknowledging that this was the man who'd called himself Neil.

Finally, the man turned around. His eyes grew big when he saw Lydia standing there, and his face turned as white as his whipped cream.

It took Lydia just a moment to place him. He'd grown thinner since high school. More pale and haggard. She hoped she contained her shocked look well enough. But she was certain of who it was.

Schooner Thomas's son.

"Hello, Bernard," she said.

"Hello, Lydia."

26

———

"I'm sorry for your loss," Lydia said as they sat down outside, in the uncomfortable heat. The backs of her bare legs were going to stick to the plastic. Gross. She'd decided against having any ice cream herself. The way her stomach was knotting she didn't think adding anything to the mix would end well.

"Thanks, I guess," Bernard said, shrugging. "No one really liked him. Me included."

"True enough," Lydia said, keeping her tone light. She so desperately wanted to directly ask Bernard if he'd killed his father, but for once, she held her tongue. "Haven't seen you since high school," she said after a moment, wanting to keep Bernard there. "How have you been doing?"

"Okay, I guess," Bernard said. "Got a bar out in Spokane," he said proudly.

Lydia knew that wasn't the truth, that he merely worked at a bar, he didn't own one. But this wasn't Neil, and she knew how to hold her tongue. Occasionally.

"That's awesome," Lydia said, pasting a big smile across her face. "I run a B&B here in town."

"The *Nip and Bud*," Neil said. "On Main Street."

Though that didn't really prove anything, it did mean he knew where she worked and lived.

"Why did you introduce yourself as my ex, Neil, to Guadalupe?" Lydia finally asked, unable to keep herself completely still.

"Eh, ex-football star. Figured I could get some kind of discount or something," Bernard said. "Even though he was an asshole. Even more stuck up than you."

Lydia blinked, surprised. She didn't remember ever teasing or putting Bernard down back in the day. He'd barely registered on her radar. "Sorry about that. But Neil had my head all turned around back then," she said.

"Unlike now," Bernard said with a conspiratorial grin.

So, Bernard had heard about the "awful" date Lydia had had with Neil the night before.

"Exactly!" Lydia said. "God, he's such a horrible human being."

"He really is," Bernard said, suddenly warming to the topic. "Him and the other jocks used to torture me in the locker room."

That actually didn't sound like Neil, but Lydia's lie-detection radar didn't have enough data for her to judge Bernard's words.

"I'm so sorry," Lydia said, laying on the sincerity. "I wish there was something I could do to make up for it."

Bernard looked her up and down. "You could buy me a beer," he suggested.

"Done," Lydia said. "Come on. Let's go to *The Cove*. It's only a block away."

Lydia wasn't about to get into a car with Bernard. She did give him a wink and a suggestive smile to get him motivated.

While she still didn't have any evidence that Bernard had

killed his father, she was going to do everything she needed in order to get it.

27

"And then, and then you know what that asshole of a father said to me?" Bernard asked. "He told me that he was cutting me off!"

Lydia nodded sympathetically and took a sip of her lukewarm beer. It hadn't been difficult to get Bernard drunk. Or to prompt him into telling stories about how awful his father had been to him.

Fortunately, Bernard was a loud drunk. Talkative. And still so very angry.

They still sat at the bar in *The Cove*, ninety minutes later. The TVs hanging from the ceiling silently showed MMA fighters performing their strangely graceful ballet of dominance. Erin, the tough, tattooed woman behind the bar, silently caught Lydia's eye before she poured Bernard another beer, seeming to understand that she was the one in charge. It was all going on her tab, after all.

Lydia had known momentary fear walking into *The Cove*. None of the cops had been there. Damn it! She'd texted Misty, who hopefully had understood her message. Lydia still couldn't afford to look around a lot, though she thought maybe she'd seen Ellis walking in.

For now, she was on her own.

"That's so unfair of Schooner! To cut you off that way," Lydia said, maintaining an easy lie of sympathy. "I mean, he was your father. He owed you, right?"

Bernard beamed at her. "Exactly!" He took another drink. "Ya know, you don't seem as stuck up as I thought."

Lydia smiled and batted her eyes at him, despite how it turned her stomach to do so. She took a deep breath.

Was that Ellis's aftershave that she smelled?

"But your ex…" Bernard's voice trailed off.

"I know, right?" Lydia said. It seemed that Bernard really hated Neil. Though Lydia didn't actually despise her ex, she and Bernard had bonded over the stupidity of Neil.

"He seemed like the perfect patsy," Bernard admitted.

Lydia kept her smile pasted onto her face. "Well, everyone knows how much he hated Principal Thomas." Finally, they were getting somewhere!

Hopefully, that was Ellis beside her. And he was smart enough to have turned on the recorder on his phone or some official police device.

"So, it would make sense that he killed my father, right?" Bernard said with a huge grin.

Lydia pretended to be shocked. "No. My ex? Would he do that?"

"He might," Bernard said smugly.

"But he's not smart enough to do something like that!" Lydia exclaimed. It never hurt playing up Neil's stupidity with Bernard. She'd learned that quickly.

Bernard winked at her. "I know. Right? Had to be someone with serious smarts to knock off the old man. Then frame the high school hero."

Lydia maintained her shocked expression, gasping. "No. Really? You didn't, did you?"

Bernard nodded proudly. "I did."

Erin behind the bar stiffened, but she maintained her place a few steps down. Maybe she was recording everything Bernard was saying as well.

Still, Lydia needed more.

"I don't believe you," she said, throwing in a pout for good measure. Could she actually get Bernard to confess? Excitement mingled with the fear clenching her belly. Goosebumps ran continuously down her spine and across her shoulders. The half a beer that she'd consumed tasted extremely flat and bitter.

"Nobody else could have done it," Bernard said with scorn dripping from his voice. "I'm the only one the old coot would have allowed into the house that late at night. He was wily, that one."

Lydia gasped again. "What happened? Did you plan to kill him? Was it all thought out?" She was so close.

Bernard sighed. He'd become mercurial as a drunk, his moods changing with every sip. "No. I hadn't meant to kill him. He just made me so frigging mad, though! When I knocked him over, and the pillow was right there, it was just so easy to put it over his face and hold him down until he stopped breathing. I'd dreamed of doing it so many times. It just felt natural, you know?"

Lydia nodded sympathetically. "He was mean to you, wasn't he?" she said. She felt the presence of someone crowding into her space, at her shoulder.

She did smell that nice spicy aftershave, after all.

"I had to do it," Bernard said. "Asshole left me no choice. I needed the money to buy the bar, so those dipshits couldn't just kick me out and fire me. I coulda made it work."

Lydia swallowed. A sense of weird calm washed over her, as if she suddenly had a glass wall between her and Bernard.

She'd found the killer.

"Why did you stab him with one of my letter openers?" Lydia said quietly. She couldn't help but ask about that.

"Cause I thought you were stuck up," Bernard said. "Figured the cops would blame the killing on you. But then I thought of Neil. I knew it would be even better to blame it on him. That's why I turned on the gas in your place. The cops could then blame him. Particularly if he suddenly showed up in town again. I hadn't meant to hurt you," Bernard said, throwing a sad-eyed look her way.

"I'm sure you didn't," Lydia said smoothly. Finally, she glanced over her shoulder.

Ellis Avery stood there. He had his phone in his hand. He'd recorded every word. He nodded to Lydia, who slid off her stool and took a step back.

Her legs shook as if she'd just run one of those ridiculous 5K marathons they had around the lake. Her gut kept twisting, turning over repeatedly. She had both the shivers as well as the sweats, her palms clammy.

"Bernard Thomson? I'm placing you under arrest," Ellis said, his deep voice carrying across the quiet of the bar.

Fortunately, Bernard stayed morose, and didn't switch over to fighting mad again. He went peacefully with the detective. All the patrons in the bar stared at the procedure. Lydia already knew the gossip mill would have a lot to talk about the next few months.

She turned to Erin, ready to settle up her tab. Erin handed back her credit card and said, "On the house. Thank you for getting that killer out of our town."

The rest of the bar suddenly stood up, applauding and cheering. Lydia didn't blush, not really. But she did feel her cheeks grow warm, as well as her heart.

This was why she'd pursued the killer so hard. Not for the cheering, but for her people, her town.

This place she called home.

28

*L*ydia woke up the next morning feeling relaxed and refreshed, despite how late she'd been up the previous night talking with her friends and neighbors. She was finally feeling settled in again, in her own place. She sailed through prep that morning with Misty setting up the front of the restaurant.

Misty came bustling into the kitchen shortly after they'd opened. Lydia already had eggs and pancakes cooking on the grill.

"Got a question for you, boss," Misty said, instead of placing the next order.

"Go ahead," Lydia said when Misty didn't continue immediately. She lifted on edge of one of the pancakes, making sure it was perfectly cooked before she flipped it.

"Seems one of the customers wants a chat with you," Misty finally replied. "Those ready?"

"In a minute or so, yeah," Lydia said. "Who is it?" Was there something wrong with one of the rooms? Had she suddenly been infested with cockroaches or something?

"Neil," Misty said. "Came in here and ordered breakfast."

That…hadn't been what Lydia had been expecting. She glanced over at Misty, puzzled.

The sour look on her co-worker's face spoke volumes. "Could refuse him service. Just say the word."

"No, it's okay. I'll go talk with him," Lydia said. She wouldn't rush out there immediately—he was going to have to wait until she'd finished cooking the current order.

She was too curious to wait in the kitchen much longer than that, though, and walked out of the kitchen soon after that.

"Hey there," she said as she approached the table.

Neil was dressed in work clothes, so he was probably on his way back to Seattle and would spend the afternoon in the office—nice suit, white shirt, blue tie.

"Seems you've cleared my name," Neil said with a smile.

Lydia waited patiently, just looking at him. Finally, she was rewarded with the words, "Thank you" actually coming out of Neil's mouth.

"You know I didn't do it for you, right?" Lydia said.

"No?" Neil said, looking confused.

"No, I did it for me," Lydia said. She couldn't help but grin. "While I was pretty sure you couldn't have killed anyone, I also knew that I was too smart to have lived, unknowingly, with a killer all those years."

Neil looked shocked for a moment before he burst out laughing. "You're really too much, you know that?"

Lydia nodded. Yes, she really was too much, at least for someone as shallow as Neil to handle.

"Still friends?" Neil said, sticking his hand out for Lydia to shake.

"Friends," Lydia said, shaking his hand. She wasn't sure what their relationship would look like in the future. However, it might be nice to at least talk on the phone with Neil sometimes. Particularly if she had a business question.

"Now, get back to the kitchen and cook me breakfast," Neil teased. "And don't let Misty spit in it."

Lydia snorted and returned to the kitchen, in many ways the heart of her business, where she got to take care of all her guests.

And one ex-husband.

29

Alice didn't work on Wednesdays. However, she still came into the restaurant that morning, with her mom, dad, and her cousin Mitch, to have breakfast together. Lydia knew that it would be a second breakfast for Jen and her husband Stu. They'd surely eaten something when the sun came up and they went out to milk the cows and take care of the rest of the livestock.

Lydia came out to say hello after making their meal, which included a special pancake for Alice that was actually three pancakes cooked together so it appeared to be a face with round ears, strawberries for eyes, and whipped cream for a large smile.

"Hi, Lydia!" Alice said as she came to their table. "Did you hear? They caught Schooner Thomas's killer! I'm no longer a person of interest."

"I did hear that," Lydia said, smiling down at her helper. "But I knew that you couldn't have done anything wrong like that."

Alice just grinned at her, while Jen nodded in her direction. "Thank you," she said quietly.

Mitch cleared his throat, drawing Lydia's attention. He was tall and thin, with straw-blond hair and a long face. His skin was pale because he never saw actual daylight. He wore large glasses over pale green eyes that seemed to make them even larger.

"So how did you determine who the killer was?" he asked in a professorial voice.

Lydia recognized that Mitch had no personal interest in her, but merely the crime itself. "It had to be whoever was impersonating Neil," she said simply.

"I'd like to talk about your deductions later," Mitch said, sounding feverish.

Lydia knew he was on that holiest of quests—novel research. "Come by later this afternoon, after three, and I'll tell you all about it." She knew there wasn't much to tell, but Mitch was going to be obsessed with her until she did.

"But that's when we're having our picnic!" Alice complained. "You should come with us instead."

Lydia paused. She knew she couldn't always be putting Alice off, it would hurt the other girl's feelings. She glanced at Jen, seeing if she could help.

"Mitch and Lydia need to talk," Jen said slowly. "And that was in part why we wanted to have the picnic, right?"

Alice's eyes grew big. "Right!" she said. "You should stay here and talk with Lydia," she declared solemnly turning to Mitch.

"Thank you for understanding," Mitch said. The smile he gave Alice transformed his face. He suddenly looked like a doting relative.

Though he held absolutely no interest to Lydia, at least she finally saw what Alice and her parents saw in him.

"This afternoon, then," Lydia said. She squeezed Alice's shoulder. "And I'll see you tomorrow!"

"Yes, I'll come to work," Alice said. "I like working with you," she added.

"Good, because I like working with you," Lydia confirmed. She smiled at all the McGowens then headed back to the kitchen to finish off the morning.

30

It wasn't until Lydia got to the Marigold room that she realized that Ellis Avery had checked out. The door was open and all his things were gone.

He'd left without saying goodbye.

Lydia tried not to be upset or disappointed. The detective didn't owe her anything. Even if she did find the killer for him. She tried to tell herself that it was a good thing. He was gone now, and her life could get back to normal.

She still found herself angrily yanking the sheets off the bed and throwing them with more force than necessary toward the open door, roughly shaking the pillows out of their cases. She was going to wash all the sheets twice, and maybe the blankets as well, just to make sure that she completely removed all trace of the detective's aftershave.

Lydia stomped around the bed, heading for the bathroom to grab the towels there, when her foot collided with a small box.

Ow.

Huh. Seemed that Ellis had gone ahead and gotten that half case of wine from Blue Pond winery.

Then left it behind.

She checked her phone, finding out that she still had the text from Sergeant Gonzales, telling her that the police were about to make the formal announcement of Schooner's death. She texted him back, letting him know that Detective Avery had left something behind, should she drop it off at the police station for him to pick it up?

It wasn't until Lydia was mostly finished with cleaning all the rooms on the third floor before her phone buzzed with a text from an unknown number.

*Will stop by Friday night to pick up
my wine*

Feeling foolish, Lydia still saved the number as *Ellis Avery, Detective* under her contacts.

And found her heart lightening when she realized that she would get to see the detective one last time.

*L*ydia refused to do anything different Friday morning. No, she was going to wear her normal hairpins and braid. A plain gray T-shirt and black shorts. Sandals. A smile. While Ed and Alan might have chided her for not at least applying a little lip gloss, Lydia would not change her appearance, or who she was, not for anyone. Least of all some man who might have dreamy eyes and nice hands and move so steadily and who lived so very far away.

She still found herself nervous as she checked her guests in, waiting for Ellis to show up on her doorstep. He hadn't specified a time when he might be there. Still, she found herself lingering in the restaurant, dusting the teapots on the wall, just so she wouldn't miss him.

When the last of Lydia's guests had checked in for the evening, it was around six PM. She was about to go and make herself something to eat when the chime above the door rang one last time.

There he was. She could tell it was him, just from the shape of his broad shoulders and how he carried himself: not overly proud like Neil, but just confident. Competent.

It was going to take a long time before she'd forget him.

"Hi, Detective Avery," Lydia said, putting down the pot she'd finished dusting for the third time.

"Ellis, please," he said, smiling softly at her. He appeared to be drinking in her appearance as well.

After a few moments of silently staring at each other, Lydia finally made herself move. "I have your half-case of wine right here," she said, walking away from him and behind the counter, pulling it out and setting it on the counter.

"Thank you," Ellis said. He put one hand on the box, as if balancing it there. "I debated just telling you to keep it. As a thank you for helping find the killer."

"And why didn't you?" Lydia asked. She found herself drawn forward, around the edge of the counter. Maybe it was something in his eyes, how deep they always appeared.

The veneer of the detective was nowhere to be seen.

"There might have been a cousin or some other relation at the station in Yakima who let me know in no uncertain terms that you were not, in fact, getting back together with your ex. That you might, instead, be amenable to dating someone else," Ellis said.

"So I have Misty to thank for your return this evening?" Lydia said. Her heart fluttered and she felt lighter than she had all week.

Ellis shrugged. "It's a small town. Word gets around."

Lydia nodded then sighed, forcing herself to stay exactly where she was standing and not get any closer. "You living in Yakima makes it a lot more difficult, you know. Plus the whole detective thing."

"I know," Ellis said. "Believe me, I've thought about those things as well. My own ex complained that I stopped being human sometimes and went all cop on her."

"I've seen it," Lydia admitted.

"I can do better," Ellis said, taking a half step closer. "You make me want to do better."

Lydia closed the distance between them. She put her hand up on Ellis's chest, amazed to find out that his heart was beating as fast as her own.

He placed one of his own warm hands against hers, pressing it harder against him.

"I can't promise forever," Lydia said. She needed to make sure that he understood that. "All I can say is that I want to take a run at it, at least try to make it work."

"That's all I can ask for," Ellis said. "And to let you know that I'll try as well."

That amazing scent of his aftershave washed over Lydia as she stepped closer, masculine and steady, like the best wood soap mixed with bay leaves. His lips were soft even as his other arm circled her waist and pulled her close.

Oh, Lydia could get used to this. Being held like this. Supported. Maybe even loved.

It was more than enough for now.

The End

ABOUT THE AUTHOR

Leah Cutter writes page-turning fiction in exotic locations, such as a magical New Orleans, the ancient Orient, Hungary, the Oregon coast, rural Kentucky, Seattle, Minneapolis, and many others.

She writes literary, fantasy, mystery, science fiction, and horror fiction. Her short fiction has been published in magazines like *Alfred Hitchcock's Mystery Magazine* and *Talebones*, anthologies like Fiction River, and on the web. Her long fiction has been published both by New York publishers as well as small presses.

Find Leah's books on Knotted Road Press at (www.KnottedRoadPress.com)

Follow her blog at www.LeahCutter.com.

Reviews

It's true. Reviews help me sell more books. If you've enjoyed this story, please consider leaving a review of it on your favorite site.

Come someplace new…
Are you a traveler? Do you enjoy exploring strange new worlds, new cultures, new people?

Journey into the various lands envisioned by Leah Cutter.

Sign up for my newsletter and I'll start you on your travels with a free copy of my book, *The Island Sampler*.

I will never spam you or use your email for nefarious purposes. You can also unsubscribe at any time.

http://www.LeahCutter.com/newsletter/

ABOUT KNOTTED ROAD PRESS

Knotted Road Press fiction specializes in dynamic writing set in mysterious, exotic locations.

Knotted Road Press non-fiction publishes autobiographies, business books, cookbooks, and how-to books with unique voices.

Knotted Road Press creates DRM-free ebooks as well as high-quality print books for readers around the world.

With authors in a variety of genres including literary, poetry, mystery, fantasy, and science fiction, Knotted Road Press has something for everyone.

Knotted Road Press
www.KnottedRoadPress.com

9 781644 701652